THE
KEY MAN

Bruce Rubenstein

**CALUMET
EDITIONS**

Minneapolis

Acknowledgments

The author wishes to acknowledge the help of several insurance experts and attorneys who must remain anonymous, but whose assistance was invaluable in respect to the research for this novel.

About the Author

Bruce Rubenstein has published hundreds of true crime stories in weeklies and monthly magazines. In 1991 he received the Chicago Bar Association's Herman Kogan Media Award for his Chicago Magazine article about the conviction of four Mexican immigrants for a quadruple homicide (dubbed "The Milwaukee Avenue Massacre" by the Sun Times) that they did not commit. They were serving the 12th year of their sentences of life without the possibility of parole when his article came out. As a result of his article the Governor of Illinois pardoned them. An anthology of his crime stories, titled Greed Rage and Love Gone Wrong, was published by the Univ. Of Minnesota Press in 2004. He won the Minnesota State Arts Council award for fiction in 1979, and published short stories in little magazines in the 70s and 80s. His story, Smoke got In My eyes, written for the Akashic Books' anthology, Twin Cities Noir (2006), was nominated for the Shamus Award. His short fiction has recently appeared in Ellery Queen's Mystery Magazine. His book about a notorious art theft, titled The Rockwell Heist was published by Borealis Press in March 2013.

THE
KEY MAN

After the Margaret Thornton fiasco I was in the dumps, but not for long. I started going to the movies on a regular basis, afternoon matinees. It was a comfort for a time, then it just got to be a habit. I'd buy a ticket and slide into the theater without bothering to look at the marquee. The film ended about the time I wanted a drink.

Sometimes Blanche Shuh came along. We disagreed about the plots—affably, but completely. It was a matter of perspective. For example, she thought the two big hits that winter, Gold Diggers of 1935 and Top Hat, were about gals finding the guy of their dreams. I thought they were about money, and how some lucky dog ended up with it—a topic of endless fascination during The Great Depression.

The only character I identified with in either film was played by Frank McHugh, a bit actor who'd have fit right in at Tin Cup's. He played the wayward son of a rich widow in Gold Diggers. The big question is whether he'll survive his run-ins with gangsters, gamblers and other hard guys, but he not only survives, he prospers. He falls for Dick Powell's fiancé, she falls for him, and the film ends with the two of them figuring how to spend mom's dough.

Blanche thought it was about McHugh's sister, played by Gloria Stuart, prying Dick Powell loose from his squeeze.

Top Hat was incomprehensible, although I picked up on an element of plot that was central to both films; the nefarious foreign weasel. I took that as a reference to current events. If there was any trouble in the world, those rats across the pond were causing it. A conniving Russian dance director tried to get his hands on the widow's fortune in Gold Diggers, but he was foiled. So was the Italian pansy in Top Hat. But before what's his name, the hoofer, finally outwits him, his dance partner almost marries the guy. Could this happen in real life? A down-to-earth Midwestern gal with legs to make a gentleman's groin stir comes within a whisker of getting hitched to a dusky-skinned deviant who can barely speak American?

Anything can happen in the movies, of course, but what usually did was a series of unlikely events leading to something predictable, if not inevitable.

I did see one tear-jerker that left me feeling like nothing else was ever possible. The poor production quality worked to its advantage. It was gray and scratchy, like something half-remembered that you'd prefer to forget completely.

It concerned an earnest young mother with an only son, and a dour, hard-drinking husband who speaks in an old country brogue when he speaks at all. Mostly he is moody and silent, even when you see him sitting in a turn-of-the century style saloon with the other Mustache Petes. The atmosphere in that joint is funereal, which is fitting, because they're all drinking themselves to death.

Many's the time mother and son go to the saloon, and drag dad out. Mom isn't allowed through the door due to her gender, so it falls on the kid. He pulls at his father's sleeve, and pleads with him—Dah, come home—but Dah stays put.

Mom goes to the priest for guidance on the Q T, and is advised to pray. It doesn't work. Awhile later, unbeknownst to mom (In movies you know things about the characters that they don't know about each other—isn't that cheating?), the kid goes to the same priest. He's maybe ten at the time.

Father, he says, I keep hopin' things'll get better, but they just get worse.—You must not despair, my boy, the priest replies. There is no greater sin than that.

So the Church is worse than useless, and the community isn't much help either. Mom's friends pity her, but they tell her that she not only has to stick it out, she's duty-bound to prolong it, by trying to save her husband from himself. Long-suffering mom doesn't have enough imagination to question the life sentence she's been handed, so she and the kid slog it out all the way to the grave with the old man. The kid is thirteen when they bury him.

From then on mom is a widow-on-the-make, but in the strait-laced, Church-approved, Hibernian fashion. This leads nowhere romantically, and creates many an awkward situation, in which the gentleman caller, the widow and the son sit around their shanty-Irish parlor like three strangers on an elevator, except the ride lasts an hour or so.

Might I call on'ye again, Mrs. McDonough? the gentleman inquires, upon leaving.

Cut to the kid's eyes rolling at that quaint anachronism. This is all told from his perspective, years later. Mom, eternally the widow, still lives in the shanty, but they don't see much of each other. As for the kid, he's grown up wary of the kind of involvements that lead to emotional responsibility. He's better-natured than his old man about drinking, but a lush nonetheless.

There weren't many films like that. Most of them were "light-hearted romps" in the parlance of the poster. The newsreels, on the other hand, were about history, which was being made a mile a minute over in Europe. Lots of Hun soldiers marching the goose-step, then a slow fade to some solemn Limey wringing his hands—Sir this, Prime Minister that—interchangeable worrywarts.

Meanwhile the Wops were fixin' to invade the Fuzzy-Wuzzys. That was supposed to concern us here, as if we didn't have enough to worry about—commies set to take over Detroit, kids dying of the dust pneumonia, a sheriff shot to death at a foreclosure auction in Iowa.

One newsreel had scenes of half-starved yokels staring in bewilderment at some neat little bungalows they were supposed to move into. They were starving Okies, being relocated to "Green Towns" in upstate New York. There was some comic relief when pa tried to screw a light bulb into the ceiling, or ma used the flush toilet to wash the clothes.

A huge celebration was held out in the desert somewhere to commemorate the completion of a 750 foot high dam, but the only ones who looked they had anything to celebrate were the politicians. Four thousand men who'd had steady work for five years were out of a job.

Unemployment overall was down to just over twenty percent, however—"a sure sign of recovery."

One February afternoon Blanche and I sat through, " A Celluloid History of The Great Depression." It began on a note of pathos; Wall Street one week after the crash, crawling with well-dressed gents peddling apples. It was enough to make you weep, unless you hate the rich or like apples. Being lukewarm about both, I tried to view it as an attempt to re-establish distribution channels in a way that put cash in empty pockets.

It occurred to me that something similar had happened here. The downtown streets, the speakeasies, and then the saloons after Prohibition was repealed, were full of flower peddlers. Hundreds of them. That was something you never saw before the crash. I gathered that it didn't happen in other cities. It was unique to St. Paul.

Who knows how things like that get started? Time marches on, in the direction it gets pointed.

A few of those posie-peddlers were the kind of geezers who had the cush in '29, but mostly they were young folks who never had much and took the Great Depression in stride. They had various ways of hawking their blossoms. There was the winsome lass on the windswept corner, the plucky kid with the patched-up knickers, and my personal favorite, the bold lad who got right in your mug when you were sparking a frail and asked if you'd like to buy the lady a flower. That was mostly a barroom phenomenon, so I saw plenty of it. The going price was only five cents a bloom so it literally took a nickel-nurser to say no. I usually managed.

This came to mind one day that Spring, when I had three chances to buy a rose on the half block walk from the spot where I'd parked my bucket, to the Criterion, where I'd arranged to meet a prospective client. That might've been a record, but it was a balmy afternoon and love was in the air—outside. Inside was the usual fug of cigarette smoke and stale beer, not as aromatic as my evening headquarters at Tin Cup's, but a relief to my jaded lungs nonetheless.

The shades were drawn against the afternoon sun. I made my way past a knot of bar flies who were clustered around their Manhattans, and settled into a booth with my back to the door—stylishly late, but nevertheless first to arrive.

There must have been a pinhole in the shade, because a moving image of the traffic on University Avenue was projected on to the back wall. It looked almost like a movie, but in color. The flivvers stretched out and floated past upside down, as if in a dream. As I watched, I idly pondered the nature of peddling—apples, flowers, information—doesn't matter. The formula is the same; buy cheap, sell dear. The recipe for acquiring the information I trade in was still simple and inexpensive—have an Irish surname and a weakness for hooch. I patted myself on the back once more for the clever way I'd turned those liabilities into assets.

Marcella Kirkwood hadn't told me much when she called. She clearly wanted to size me up before we came to terms. Other than that I didn't know what to expect, but a odd skill I've developed gave me a clue just before I saw her. A certain solid sound her heels made on the parquet floor led me to believe that she'd be a real tomato. I'd honed the knack of hearing what dames looked like by dint of much trial and error, and was rarely wrong.

"Martin McDonough?" she inquired.

Right again. I stood and asked her join me.

She was tall and smartly dressed, in a pleated skirt, a linen jacket and a ruffled white blouse open at the neck. A pair of pince nez specs dangling from a chain around her neck rested on her bosom. She had long legs, big brown eyes and penciled eyebrows. Her chestnut hair was swept into a pile, tied into a thick braid and done up in a bun, leaving her lovely face framed by naught but her nibbly pink ears. She was thirtyish, and she sported a monstrous diamond on the third finger of her left hand.

"Drink?" I asked, when she'd settled in.

"A little early, isn't it?" she replied, with a frown. "You a soak, McDonough?"

"Ah, that's harsh. But now'ya mention it, hooch is a professional hazard. I spend a lot of time loosening tongues. That's what I'm good at."

"So I've heard....hmm. Ginger ale for me."

I waved the waiter down. Dream buckets oozed across the wall behind her. We exchanged what one might call pleasantries. By the time my beer and her soft drink arrived she'd satisfied herself that we could do business.

"I want to know who murdered my father," she said. "He's been dead for a year, no arrests, nothin'. Seems like an easy case to me."

"Why's that?"

"I'm not tellin' you. I don't want to prejudice your inquiry."

That was a first. I usually have to discourage clients from actively steering my investigation, either to save money or serve some agenda. Things were going well enough professionally that I could afford to be principled.

"Your choice, but I charge by the day," I told her. "The more you tell me, the faster things usually go."

"That's ok, I've made up my mind."

I sighed. "Gonna give me the victim's name? I can tell by that manacle on your digit it wasn't Kirkwood."

She wouldn't smile but her eyes crinkled a bit.

"Robert Tuttweiler. Everybody called him Bobby."

"I'm gonna ask you to write that down, and a few other things—"

She immediately opened her purse and pulled out a pencil. "Got somethin' to write on?"

"—but first I want to know why you think the coppers aren't pursuing it."

"I told you, I don't want to prejudice your investigation."

"I'm not asking who you think the killer is. Why aren't the cops looking? That's what I want to know."

She put the pencil down, picked up her glass, squinted at it. That big rock of her's caught the flux of light coming through the pin hole, and the wall behind her went blank.

"It's not 'the cops,'" she said. "It's this one copper. Eddy Guilfoyle."—She jiggled her glass. The ice tinkled.

Evidently I was supposed to drag information out of her one piece at a time.

"Why isn't he pursuing it?"

"Because he's *corrupt*, that's why."

Of course he was corrupt, but she made it sound supremely disgusting, and she had a defiant look on her puss as she said it too, as if it were my fault. This was 1935, remember, the waning days of the layover, but gangsters were still allowed to take refuge in St. Paul if they paid off the police. That was what made life interesting in the Saintly City. How it affected the work of an investigator like Eddy Guilfoyle might make a fascinating inquiry, but in this situation it only confused things.

"As far as your father's murder is concerned, Mrs. Kirkwood, who'd want to corrupt Eddy, and why?"

"He's just *corrupt*." She wrinkled her nose as she uttered that awful word. "You can call me Marcie."

I took all of that under advisement. Being on first name terms with this lovely creature would certainly spice things up, but her theory was nonsense. The way corruption worked in St. Paul served to isolate it from ordinary people. If anything it made their lives more comfortable. The gangsters had to keep their noses clean while they were in town, and it gave the Krauts and other heathen an excuse to blame Mick coppers on the take whenever a crime went unpunished.

How did Marcie know Eddy was *corrupt*? She'd long suspected it, she explained, but about a week earlier she'd barged into the Rice Street Precinct House and demanded to know why an arrest hadn't been made.

"He couldn't look me in the eye," she said. That cinched it for her.

"Did you know that most murders go into the books unsolved?" I asked.

"No," she admitted.

"The coppers aren't exactly eager to get the word out. Fact is, they get enough evidence for a conviction in maybe three outta ten."

She was unmoved. "Most of'em aren't as easy as this one," she said.

Try as I might, I couldn't get anything more out of Marcie. I settled for the names of her mother, sister and brother, their address and phone number, and the advance on my fee. She extracted the promise of frequent progress reports in return.

"I want to see if you're getting the picture," she said.

I could hardly wait. I was half in love with every tomato I met back then, but I rarely encountered anything like Marcie. 'Classy' was an overworked adjective during the Depression, but it certainly fit her. Every head in the joint turned when she left. She had hips about as wide as her shoulders, and that long, lazy hourglass between.

I dug up a smidgin of dope about the murder that evening at Tin Cup's.

"Bobby Tuttweiler?" said little Mikey Bailey, a bull with a local beat that included a few blocks of Hun turf over in St. Albert's parish. "Some Mocky dropped him, that's what I heard."

I bought him a drink and prodded, but to no avail.

"Tell the truth it didn't make much of an impression," he said. "Mocky ices a Hun—so what? Didn't happen on my shift. Some dame comes into his shop early in the morning t'buy flowers, finds him dead. Talk to Eddy Guilfoyle. He was the investigator."

A fight broke out and interrupted us or I would've asked a few more questions. Fights are hardly a rarity at Tin Cup's, but I remember that as an especially combative evening. This particular tussle involved a Kraut posey-pusher who had the temerity to stick his nose in the door and holler "ROSES," and one of Slapper Doran's stable of young prize fighters, a middleweight named Harry Cassidy.

The Hun tried to put his bouquet in front of his face to protect himself, but this Cassidy had a quick straight left and he landed it hard.

The Hun dropped his blossoms, and commenced swinging, a ballsy move that those of us at the bar approved vociferously. It had the makings of an interesting brawl, but Doran broke it up. That was unlike him. Doran was a pushy, loudmouthed little guy who got in the fight business so he could surround himself with boxers and act tough, or so it seemed to me. He usually encouraged his boys to throw hands when an excuse presented itself. It saved gym expenses.

Doran sat the Hun down at his table, took a handkerchief out of his breast pocket, and dabbed at the Hun's bloody nose. He made Cassidy pick up the flowers, waved the waitress down and bought the kid a drink. Soon they were all getting along famously, as young guys will after they've expended a burst of energy in a wholesome way. Before I lost interest, I noticed Doran take his wad out of his pocket and purchase the flowers. Later on he was walking around giving roses to all the frails. The Hun was long gone by then.

Next afternoon I stopped by The Real McKay's office, and asked if he'd ever heard of Bobby Tuttweiler.

"Yeah," he replied. " A genuine Lothario. Sheila Delaney dumped me when she got involved with him."

"'Lothario?'"

He handed me a dictionary. His machine buzzed, and began spitting out tape.

Weeping Widows

A couple days later I met Marcie for an update. Not at a hot sheet joint as I'd been fantasizing. At the Criterion again. By then I'd spoken to mom and sis, who told me nothing, and a few of my copper pals, who were the usual fount of information.

The waiter said hello, and seated me in a back booth. He must've assumed we were lovers meeting on the sly. The Criterion had become famous for that since Prohibition ended.

Nearby sat another type of customer the joint was known for. Middle-aged women found it a comfortable spot for a solitary drink. They were treated respectfully, and gentlemen sometimes sent the waiter over with an offer to buy one, which could be accepted or politely turned down. Genteel ladies all, but not necessarily candidates for sainthood. Much of the scuttlebutt that spiced up everyday life in our little city, and occasionally found its way into the gossip columns, owed its existence to the peculiar acoustics of the Criterion.

"I know where you get your looks," I said, after Marcie turned down my offer of a drink.

"Oh? Where."

"Your mother."

"Bang-up, Martin." She placed her pince nez on her nose and peered at me intently. "You're a real sleuth."

"An observation, that's all."

"Any observations about dad's murder? Or am I here so you can look at me."

"Little of each."

She dropped the specs. Her mouth retained its stern line but her eyes crinkled again, and I couldn't help noticing she'd worn lipstick for the occasion. Hope springs eternal.

"So what 'd you find out?" she asked.

"That your father was the greatest flower salesman ever lived. That every florist in St. Paul bought from Midland Wholesale Flowers when he was their salesman, and a few months before he was killed, he quit, opened his own business and took all his accounts with him. Which made the owner of Midland pretty unhappy."

She raised a pencilled brow. "Bingo," she said.

I could see her point, but something her mother told me, a mere aside as I was leaving, led me to believe it wasn't quite so clear cut.

****

Bob had the most beautiful funeral," Betty Tuttweiler had informed me, but as she described it, she spoke caustically of a dozen or so sobbing women "hiding behind veils," who'd elbowed their way into the inner circle as the coffin was being lowered, and thrown bouquets of roses into the grave.

"There were so many weeping widows you'd have thought he was a bigamist," she said. "But I guess that was the nature of the business. Women do most of the buying for retail florists, so Bob saw a lot of them."

Marcie's sister Angie, who'd been bustling around putting the final touches on her makeup before going out for the evening, stopped in her tracks and gave mom a bemused look.

"What?" Betty asked.

Angie just shook her head.

I'd let their little interchange pass without further inquiry, but I decided to mention it to Marcie.

"Let me put this as tactfully as possible. Think maybe a jealous husband might be worth a look?"

"No."

"Oh. I'll keep that in mind."

I told her about Mikey Bailey's tip.

"Sounds like you're on to somethin' there," she said. "Don't pay much attention to mom and Angie. They're tired of the whole thing. Mom won't even talk to me about it."

I'd sensed as much, although they were gracious and friendly. Real friendly. Betty was tall, fifty or so, but quite the looker still. She knitted her hands as we spoke, more beleaguered-seeming than nervous. It made me want to put an arm around her, which wouldn't have been hard. The moment I walked in she seated me on the sofa and sat down next to me.

"Angie, bring the pictures," she said.

Soon Angie squeezed in on the other side, photo album in hand. Betty flipped through and showed me a photo of her late husband. He had that lounge-lizard look, right down to the half-smile and the curl of smoke from the cigarette gripped like a dart between his thumb and forefinger. He had a hawk nose, and eyes that you just knew were blue, even though the picture was sepia-toned; intense, snapping eyes, hooded under thick, dark eyebrows. A lick of hair hung over his forehead.

"Handsome, wasn't he," said Angie. She leaned in close to tap her finger on the photo. I felt her breath on my shoulder. My leg pressed up against Betty's. Heat came off both of them in waves. It was about seven in the evening of what had been a very warm day. The light from the lowering sun through the living room window shone red through a scrim of dust bowl haze. The air in the house hardly stirred.

"We're alone here now," Betty said. "Bobby Junior comes in late at night, sleeps all day. Oh, I don't know..." Her fidgety hands brushed against mine, which were braced against my thighs.

"Uh, do'ya feel, well...safe?" I asked.

"How can we?" Betty replied. "With Bob being shot and all."

"I do," said Angie. She gave me a quick smile. "Not that it wouldn't be nice to have a guy around sometimes. My brother is gone a lot."

"Oh sure, you feel safe," said Betty. "You don't sit here alone at night wondering where your children are, when they're coming -"

Angie leaned over me to put her hand on her mom's arm. "We're not kids, ma," she said. "We're fine, you'll be fine."

I was rigid and sweaty, trying hard not to cop a feel, wondering why I was trying so hard. Nobody else was. Angie braced her hand on my knee when she reached across me. I could smell her hair. She wasn't lean and statuesque like Marcie. More the round, scrumptious type.

"Hot, isn't it?" she said. "Want some lemonade or somethin', Martin?"

"Nah, I'm ok. Well, maybe."

"Get him some, dear," said Betty.

She brought me a glass of iced lemon drink, then continued to bustle about while her mother and I spoke, passing close enough for me to get another whiff of her perfume (nice but not subtle) and a touch or two from the fringe of her shimmy skirt. Her cheeks dimpled when she smiled. She was certainly easy on the eye, even if she didn't have legs to the chin like mom and sis.

"You ever hafta kill a guy, Martin?" she asked.

"Naw, never came to that."

"Marcie told me she wanted to hire you," Betty said. "I wish she hadn't. It's time to put it behind us, don't you think?"

"It's easier when y'know who did it. Or so they say."

"But that's not going to happen, is it." Her tone was resigned.

"We'll see. Marcie claims the investigator's the problem. Says he's bent. What do you think?"

"Eddy? He's a dear."

I knew Eddy. He wasn't a dear.

I got some idea of what the deceased was like from talking with them, but not much else. They made it clear who'd run the show in their family. Angie said her social life was more to her liking now that she didn't have to feign interest in various well-born stiffs just to please dad. Betty wouldn't discuss the murder. Angie seemed to take her cues from her mom.

I asked when I might find Bobby Junior home. Betty said call first and I'd catch him sooner or later. When I rose to leave, Angie asked if she could have a ride. She was headed down to Kuby's joint.

"They have live music there now," she said.

She was bubbly on the way. She told me she loved jazz music. I said I was surprised they had smokes playing at Kuby's. Only one, she explained, the rest of the band were guys she knew from the neighborhood. I gathered they were Krauts like her. Playing jazz music. Strange times we live in.

"Wanna tell me who killed your father?" I asked.

She shook her head. "You'll find out soon enough."

"Marcie tell you to clam up?"

She admitted she had, but explained that none of them, especially her mother, needed much coaxing. They were keenly disappointed that a case that they thought would be solved in a few days was a year old, and had apparently hit a dead end. Like her sister, she assumed I would draw the obvious conclusion once the facts were revealed.

"Thanks," she said, when I dropped her off. "You know

how to get hold'a me. Say hi to Marcie." She squeezed my hand before leaving.

****

"Angie says 'hi,'" I told her big sister, who barely acknowledged that she'd heard. She told me I should have gone into Kuby's with Angie if I wanted to talk to her brother.—"He spends most of his time there," she said.

"You worried about him?" I asked, just to keep the conversation moving. I didn't want her to leave.

"He took dad's death pretty hard."

"He into the hooch now?"

She shrugged. "Bobby's a poet or somethin'," she said, as if that answered the question.

Mom and Angie's feelings seemed a more promising line of inquiry anyway, so I inquired.

"Why do you want to know?" she asked. Her attitude was that I shouldn't let anything distract me from the obvious, but I persisted.

"It was a jolt when he was killed," she told me "but it was a relief to have him gone, if you must know. He had ideas about how we should live our lives, and he was kind of a tyrant about some things.—Buy me a drink. Put it on the bill if you want."

Needless to say, that was a welcome development. I assured her the drinks were on me. She ordered a Manhattan.

"I take it your father cheated," I said.

"Boy, did he." At long last she smiled for real. On top of everything else she had that sexy gap between her two front teeth.

"Who did he cheat with?"

"Every gal he could, till the day he died. That dame who found him? Guess what she came to the shop for."

"To buy flowers?"

"Ha!—Well, that's not fair. Most of his sweeties bought flowers from him. That was the excuse he used when him and mom argued."

She sloshed her drink around, took a sip.

"I loved my dad, but he *corrupted* us."

There was that word again. This time I asked her to explain.

"Everybody thinks about two-timin'," she said. "Doin' it, that's different. Dad turned mom into a cheat. It didn't come naturally to her like it did to him, but she's a number, always was, so she had plenty of opportunity. They pretended things were ok in front of us kids, then argued when they thought we couldn't hear. That's how I grew up. By the time Angie and me were in high school they didn't care if we heard or not. My brother was still a kid. We'd take him out and play with him so he wouldn't have to listen."

"Maybe your mom killed him."

"Not funny."

"Wasn't a joke."

I waited for her to react. She didn't.

"I still don't see why you're so sure a jealous husband didn't do it," I said. "Seems logical to me."

She shook her head. "You didn't know my dad. People loved him. We loved him, in spite of it all. Mom loved him, the gals he played around with loved him. Their husbands probably loved him. He was handsome, smart, witty, a great salesman, took the parish orphan kids on outings."

"Sounds perfect."

"But he wasn't. He used animal magnetism to get what he wanted. That was his flaw."

"It's human nature."

"But it's not much of an example. Dad was a liar too, lied like a rug. Not that he was ashamed. He just wanted to avoid scenes. Mom had her ways of findin' out though. She liked to catch him, then use it as an excuse to tell him about her latest romance. Me'n Angie lied all the time when we were kids. About school, about our boy friends. To the priests. I didn't make an honest confession until I left home."

"That wasn't a problem for me," I told her. "I just stopped goin' to confession. All those impure thoughts.—You said everybody thinks about playin' around. That mean you too?"

"Don't be coy." She swallowed some more of her Manhattan.

"Ok. You think about playin' around with me?"

"Sure. You're handsome, you have kind of an intriguing life, a reputation. But I'd never do it."

"Aww."

She laughed and patted my hand. "Don't take it personal.—What do you need me for anyway? You meet lots of 'dames,' have lots of rumble seat sex, don't you? I suppose you're quite the rogue, Martin, a real seducer. Just like dad."

I didn't know exactly where this was going, but I knew where I hoped it was going.

"From what I've gathered, I'm not in your old man's league."

"Huh." She fussed with her pince nez, and didn't say anything for awhile. -"So tell me about them," she said. "Your girl friends."

"Jeez, Marcie. They're all different. You know that."

"Ok. Tell me about one of'em."

"There's Blanche Schuh. Every once in awhile we get a yen just lookin' at each other. At least I do. She must too, because we go somewhere and—uhh .."

"God! She should restrain herself."

"Why?"

"Because nice girls—"

"Blanche isn't a nice girl, Marcie. She's a 'dame.'"

I told her about another gal, Jeannie Hallgren, former maid-in-waiting at the court of Boreas, King of the St, Paul Winter Carnival. Jeannie ran off with His Majesty a few years later.

"Quite the 'tomato' was she?" said Marcie.

She actually said 'tomato' in quotes, but I don't know who she was quoting. Not me. I'm careful how I talk around classy dames.

"You know how they choose those gals. The Snow Queen is somebody whose daddy has bucks, but the Princesses and Maids are there because they're lookers. Jeannie, well—how should I put it—Jeannie put the carnal into carnival. "

"Was she as good-lookin' as me?"

I said no, although she was in her own way,

"Damn right." She took a sip of her drink. "So, how'd you seduce her."

"I didn't. She seduced me."

"No!"

"Yeah."

I began an abbreviated version of a complicated story. I'd been hired to find the kidnapers who'd snatched the former King. His father-in-law, a prominent banker, paid the ransom, but his Majesty was never seen again.

"Oh, married was he?" Marcie interjected. "I suppose Miss whatshername lured him to his fate."

Hush, I told her, because the walls have ears at the Criterion.

"I'll tell'ya what happened if you swear you'll keep it under your hat.—I'm serious. If the so-called widow ever gets wind of what I'm about to tell'ya it would break her heart. I'm not gonna give you any names, but there are plenty of people who could put two and two together."

She swore she'd never tell a soul. I made her swear twice.

"I don't betray client's confidences," I said. "I'm not kiddin'. This is important to me."

"Ok, ok," she said.

I explained the trail of marked bills that led to Crane Lake up in northern Minnesota, and the supposed kidnapper. Who did I find? King Boreas himself, who'd connived his own disappearance and collected the ransom. He was off hunting. Jeannie invited me to spend the night before I went back.

"Ha," Marcie laughed. "Poor thing was stuck all alone in the middle of nowhere. No wonder she invited you to bed. She was scared."

I didn't bother explaining that Jeannie Hallgren was one tough cookie. I got back to the main point.

"Uh-uh, she was just lookin' for a good time. You gonna tell me somethin' like that never crosses your mind?"

She gave me a sly, sideways look.

"I told'ja it did, remember? But that doesn't mean we're gonna do it. Banish the thought."

"Why not?" I persisted.

"Because I have a good marriage, that's why.—Don't get me wrong. Dirk isn't a very *interesting* guy. I mean, he never was—never knew interesting people, never did interesting things. He'd talk about all these 'adventures' him and his friends had, but all they ever did was get blotto and speed around in their roadsters. I went with'em sometimes. There was always lotsa hooch, and you wondered if you were gonna get in an accident. Other than that it was—I don't know....dull."

"So how come you married him? Cake in the oven?"

"Uh uh." She didn't seem shocked that I'd asked.

"So—why?"

"Maybe I'll tell'ya some time, Martin. When we know each other better."

"Well, what better way to get acquainted -"

"Uh-uh." She shook her finger at me, but her eyes crinkled when she did it. She was most of the way through her Manhattan by then. "And don't say my husband wouldn't find out. That has nothin' to do with it.—Well, almost nothin'. I mean if we were on a desert island..."

I reached across the table and took her hand. "How about if we were at the St. Francis Hotel?"

She looked deep into my bloodshot blue eyes, and said, "Forget it."

I ran my thumb over that rock of hers.

"Ok, a desert island. You can use this to signal ships at sea when we get tired'a foolin' around."

She smiled again, which was all the more fetching now that I'd seen that gap between her teeth. She wouldn't sit still for another Manhattan though.

"Until my next report," I said as we parted.

The Key Man

The prospect of another meeting certainly speeded the probe. That very evening I wedged my way up to the bar next to the nefarious Eddy G, bought him one, and observed him carefully as we sipped our drinks.

He'd aged a bit, to put it mildly. Sallow skin, thinning hair, baggy eyes. *Corrupt* was an understatement. He appeared to be decomposing.

"How's it goin,' Eddy?" I inquired.

"So so."

"What'cha been up to?"

"Nothin' special."

Was it my imagination, or was he more taciturn than usual? I decided not to beat around the bush. He just shook his head wearily when I told him the subject of my inquiry.

I let him brood for awhile, and listened to Ruth Etting belt out Ten Cents A Dance on the Mighty Wurlitzer. A little too heartfelt for my taste, but her voice was compelling, so much so that the normal bar noise toned down as she sang. I suppose everyone was thinking about the same thing I was as they listened. All those newspaper stories about Etting's gangster-ex shooting her squeeze in a jealous rage.

"That dame'll never leave me alone," Eddy finally said. "I wish I'd never heard'a that case."

"What dame?"

"The deceased's daughter, of course. Who else would've hired you? The rest of the family accepted it. Other day she chased me down at the precinct. Called me a highbinder in so many words. It was embarrassing fr'christ's sake."

"I had no idea you were so sensitive, Eddy."

"Ah, go to hell," he muttered.

He drained his drink and started to walk away, but, presto! I was my normal cajoling self again. He didn't exactly cheer up, but he succumbed to the point where he gave me the straight dope, in detail.

"Deceased had a shop down the street by St. Albert's, a storefront with a big cooler where he kept some stock. He was usually there by six A M, opened at seven, which I come to find out is how it's done in the flower business. The retail florists do all their buyin' early in the morning. He had an appointment at seven, a woman. She arrives a few minutes before, thinkin' she'll knock on the door but sees it's open. Walks in, finds Tuttweiler lyin' behind the counter. Face looks like hamburger. Somebody put a twelve-gauge with a load of birdshot right under his chin and let him have both barrels. Little tiny BBs. Wouldn't'a killed him at ten feet."

Eddy was warming to his story. He was neglecting his drink. Some color had returned to his mug. The redder he got the better he looked, relatively speaking. On his best day he resembled nothing so much as a stubbed toe. His puss looked like a normal face viewed upside down—nose like a big square chin, underbite, little porcine eyes too, but that beezer of his defined him. It looked like it had withstood many a solid punch and about five shots of whiskey a day for decades.

He was a good investigator though, and the things he highlighted as he described the murder scene—the weapon, the fact that no money had been taken, the fact that the cooler was open and an armful of freshly cut roses lay on the floor next to the body—added up the same way for him that they did for me: Bobby Tuttweiler opened his door for someone before business hours, most likely someone who came under the guise of doing business, and that person killed him. His wallet was still in his pocket and the cash drawer was untouched, so robbery wasn't the motive. Nor was it a professional drop. Droppers don't lug shotguns around, especially if they're loaded with ammo that wouldn't be fatal unless you practically stuck the barrel in the victim's mouth.

"The way his mush was massacred, that tell you anything?" I asked.

"Jealous girl friend? Uh-uh. I talked to the dames he was known to be intimate with. Busy man, Mr. Tuttweiler, but they all had alibis and so did their hubbys. I did the basics, Martin. Talked to the deceased's business associates, checked the whereabouts of his family. Wife and daughter were home when it happened, coppers got'em outta bed to tell'em about the murder. Son spent the night at a friend's place. Him, couple guys, some rich gal who hung out with'em, all of'em cuttin'a rug after Kuby's closed. Coppers hadda wake them up too. Bobby Junior broke down an'cried when they told him. There's only one real suspect, and he got away with it clean. Betty and her other kids accepted it, and what's her name, Marcella, sooner or later she'll have to accept it too."

"His ex-employer, right?"

"Right. Mocky name'a Sheldon Slansky, owned Midland Wholesale Flowers. Deceased quit, opened his own shop, and took every nickel'a business with him when he left. Slansky was after him to come back, makin' offers, threats. He was desperate."

"Must'a been to come up with a plan like that. What's he gonna do, march him back to his old job at gunpoint? Follow him around with a shotgun while he called on customers?"

Eddy sighed. "I'm gonna tell you what I told the Chief, what I told the prosecutors. Then I never wanna hear about this again, ok?"

He explained that Slansky had taken out an insurance policy on Bobby Tuttweiler when Bobby first began talking about leaving. It was a type of insurance called a "key man policy." It paid Slansky ten thousand dollars if his star salesman died or became disabled.

"But he quit first, so it was worthless, right?" I said.

"No. Here's the strange thing. Once the company sells the policy they can't cancel it, as long as the policy hold-er pays the premiums. Agent told me the only rule is, he couldn't'a wrote it in the first place unless the insured was an employee at the time. The insurance company figures anyone who buys a key man policy will stop payin' premiums if the key man quits workin,' but Slansky didn't stop and nobody could make him. Deceased tried, deceased's wife tried, insurance agent tried. He just told'em, 'screw you.' Paid monthly, right on time. Even though his business was goin' under."

"And he collected all that do re mi?"

"All that and more. Double the face value because it was murder. Slansky's lawyer demanded payment. The insurance company asked the D A if Slansky was gonna be indicted. D A says no, company pays Slansky twenty thousand smackers. Now who d'you think killed him?"

"I see who had motive. What else you got?"

"Opportunity. Betty Tuttweiler tells me Bobby wanted to end the bad blood between him and Slansky. Says if Slansky knocked on the door and gave Bobby some song and dance about needin' roses for his business that day he'd have said ok. Bobby goes into the cooler to get the flowers, Slanksy pulls the shotgun out from under his coat and kills him when he comes back."

"Good theory. What else?"

"Nothin.' Slansky says he was home with the wife. She backs him up. They're both lyin.' No confession, no physical evidence. Haven't found the weapon. We got motive. We got opportunity. I've seen men convicted on less, but they won't even indict him."

As his story wound down Eddy deflated like a tire with a slow leak. By the time he finished he was pale as a ghost again. I asked him why they wouldn't prosecute, a topic he would've certainly discussed with the D A. He shrugged and mumbled something about Slansky's lawyer.

"You don't have any of that money, do'ya?" I asked.

"What the hell do you think?"

"Just touchin' all the bases before I slide home."

He sighed. "Don't think it's the first time I been asked," he said.

Before we parted he inquired if I'd been attending mass recently.

"Nah, I'm fallen away, Eddy."

"Go back to Holy Mother, Martin," he advised. "It's the only comfort we have."

That and his appearance led me to believe the iron crab had him. I made a mental note to remember Eddy the next time I prayed. If he lived that long.

At that point the murder of Bobby Tuttweiler appeared to be a routine case of know but can't prove. One thing bothered me though. As Eddy noted, stir is full of men convicted on motive and opportunity alone, so why wasn't Slansky prosecuted?

It wasn't exactly inexplicable. The D A doesn't want to lose a case, so he's loathe to go to court without a confession or some solid evidence. But the people who elected him grumble about the streets of St. Paul being full of gangsters who appear to be immune from prosecution, which they are. Given the popular clamor, somebody has to go to trial some time. A Mockey who murders a Kraut for money seems like a good candidate. Hotshot lawyer or no, why not put him in front of a jury and roll the dice?

I knew who to ask, and I wasn't going to run into him at Tin Cup's. Teddy Eccles and I were freshmen at St. Thomas together. Like me, Teddy entered college determined to follow in his father's footsteps. Difference was, his father was a judge and mine was a lush. Teddy was headed for law school, I was headed for the door but I did enjoy my year of higher education. My favorite course was Sacred Music, which baffled Teddy because I couldn't play a note on any instrument, still can't, nor can I carry a tune. Something— scales and melodic lines, the way sound evoked emotion —struck a chord in my impressionable young mind—but I digress. I lasted two semesters, during which Teddy and I spent a lot of time together, mostly in joints where they played dixieland jazz.

Teddy served a short apprenticeship in the D A's office, then made a career of defending guys the D A prosecuted. It was his idea that I become a private eye. I was contemplating joining the police force (actually, now that I think of it, Uncle Jerk was pressuring me to join the police force and I was contemplating whether I wanted to spend my life being a copper), but Teddy said that with my connections and my knack for using them I'd do better on my own.

"And it's a good way to meet women," he added, which cinched it for me.

Teddy was obviously my next move, but there's more than one way to prejudice an inquiry. I was determined to go after this case one step at a time, with frequent reports to my client. It was still the shank of the evening when I left Tin Cup's and headed for Kuby's joint to find Bobby Jr.

Mr. Kuby's horizons had expanded recently. It began with the installation of the Mighty Wurlitzer. The day time regulars like Jerk and a few other old gents grumbled, but it didn't change things much for them. After dark, however, Kuby's became a juke joint. First I heard there was live music was when Angie told me, but I knew it was hot spot for the young crowd.

A four piece band was blaring away when I walked in. They were set up on a little stage in back that was well lit compared to the rest of the place, and sure enough, they had a smoke piano player. There were couples jitterbug dancing on the sawdust covered floor. I grabbed the last empty stool at the bar and looked around for Angie, but couldn't make out faces. She spotted me though.

"MARTIN," she shouted to be heard over the music. 'WHAT BRINGS YOU HERE?"

She squeezed in beside me. Her hip rubbed against mine. I stood quickly, and offered her my seat without thinking. She took it and set her drink in front of her like it was the most natural thing in the world. Apparently Kuby's after dark was the kind of joint where a frail could sit at the bar. At least Angie could. I didn't see any others.

The stage lights dimmed. The band put their instruments down and drifted out to the murky dance floor, among them the smoke, who was practically invisible except for a derby hat that he wore with a fat red ribbon tied around it. A ceiling fan was stirring up enough breeze so the ribbon hovered and squirmed like the tail of a kite above the milling crowd.

I told Angie I was hoping to talk to her brother. "He was here a few minutes ago," she said. "Don't see him now though."

"Too bad. Gotta cross him off my list."

I tried to get the bartender's attention, which took awhile. By the time I turned back a couple of fellows were standing next to her.

"Martin McDonough, meet Danny Wegleitner," said Angie.

It was the rose peddler who'd stuck his beezer into Tin Cup's and got punched. We shook hands.

"And this's my brother Bobby," she said.

Even in the dim light and nothing to go by but the photo I'd seen, I could tell he was the spit and image of his father. Same nose, same black hair, same blue eyes, though his were gentle and melancholy, not full of snap like the old man's. He had a strange outfit on; creased black pants, red suspenders, frayed white shirt, and a bow tie hung loose around his open collar.

We shook hands, awkwardly for him, because a tomato was clinging to his arm, a real dish of a blonde.

"This's Amy," he said, jerking his head in her direction.

Amy nodded without tearing her adoring gaze from Bobby Jr. She was a gorgeous, dissolute-looking young thing, barely of an age to be in a saloon.

"Got a few bucks, sis?' he asked Angie. "I left my cush in my other pants."

"You'd leave your head home if it wasn't attached to your neck," said Angie— fondly, the way you'd chastize a beloved pet who'd just peed the floor again. She opened a little sequined handbag and pulled out a bill. I spotted a deck of Luckys in there. Angie was quite the bearcat, no question. She waved at the bartender.

"Allow me," I said, more out of self-interest than civility.

They ordered straight gin. Given the music and the general tenor of the joint, I took that as an homage to the late Bix Beiderbecke, a noted gin drinker, and if memory serves, the wayward son of a Kraut music teacher. Amy and the other kid (they called him "Wigger") attacked theirs with gusto. Bobby was a sipper.

"Told'ja about Martin, remember?" said Angie to her brother.

"Yeah. Marcie hired him to find out who killed Dad." It looked for a moment like he might weep.

"Aww Bobby," said Amy. She gave him a quick hug.

I waited to ask a few questions in private, but some gals began to gravitate around, a few fellows followed, and soon I could see there was no way to cut Bobby loose. Angie joined their conversation. She caught me glancing at her and shot me a smile. A pained look crossed Wigger's mug.

Dick Pranke, the guy who'd fingered Baby Face Nelson for Jack back in '34, was hovering on the edge of the crowd. He didn't look like he belonged there. He was older than the rest, more my age.

Pranke was maybe five foot five, but he had a big head crowned with a shock of reddish hair, a moon face, and great

big hands that he waved around and gestured with constant-
ly. He had a big, toothy smile on his mug that appeared to be
meant for someone in particular, but I had nothing better to
do than observe him and I could see that it wasn't. He was
gassing with everybody at once, and he'd look from one to
the other without ever altering that expression.

He had a big chin for a little guy too. The same kind of
chin as that wop who'd been strutting around the newsreels
lately. Pretty soon he recognized me.

"Hey, Martin, what brings you here?"

"Business.—This your hangout?"

"Lately. I try to keep movin." He gave me a little nudge,
like that was a gag and I was in on it. "These kids come
from all over town t'hear this coon music. Streetcars ain't
runnin' by the time the joint closes. Some of'em buy used
buckets from me."

He felt out my need for wheels. I told him my Model
A was running ok, and would for awhile because one of
the guys at Mrs. Dunn's boarding house liked to work on
cars. We gabbed a little about the fights, then he excused
himself.—"Gotta see a man about a dog," he said.

The smoke from the band wandered over, a tall, power-
ful-looking guy, with skin so black it was blue. He might've
been around my age too, but it's hard to tell with those people. I asked him where he was from. Chicago, he told me,
but some friends who worked on the trains had told him
about an opportunity here in St. Paul.

"You play in any'a the hot bands in Chicago?"

"Nosuh. I labored in obscurity, amongst the oxford gray."

I smiled. He smiled back.

"What we grinnin' 'bout, my ofay friend?" he inquired.

"Way you talk reminds me of someone I met at a club over in Minneapolis. A horn player."

You could almost see his ears prick up. "Who?"

"Lester somethin, ' Lester..."

"You heard Lester Young?"

"Yeah, that's the name."

"Prez my man! Prez my idol! He be talkin' with a 'lithp' sometime, correct?"

"That's him."

I bought him a whiskey, a selection that made us a minority of two. I told him I was a private eye looking into the murder of Bobby Tuttweiler's father. He'd heard about it.

"Happened around the time I come here," he said.- "That guy a friend'a yours?" He nodded in Pranke's direction, and referred to him by a nickname I didn't quite catch.

"Just an acquaintance. What'd you call him? 'Duce'?"

"'Dutchy.' Folks here call him Dutchy. —Man so crooked he could piss around a corner."

Turns out Pranke sold him a used Model T, said it was a runner, charged him a C note.

"First cold day, turn the crank, motor goin' 'ruhhh-ruh-hh-ruhhh' real slow-like. Never did spark. Told Dutchy, but he jus' say 'bad break.'—'Bad break' hell. Jack-roll is what it was."

We commiserated about car salesmen and cold weather. He told me in more detail why he'd come here. Some Pullman porter friends of his had tipped him that white youngsters in St. Paul were evincing an interest in hot music. The porters stayed in the Rondo neighborhood during layovers, and the white kids had been frequenting a blind pig across the street from their rooming house.

"The oxford boys came for the jazz. An' the muggles. An' the gash." He swiped the back of his hand across his beezer. "Not to mention the nose candy."

The porters made extra swag peddling the stuff, he explained.

This wasn't exactly news to me. The cursed Sunday closing laws in our state—a veritable sea of sanctimony dotted about with islands of honest self-indulgence—had driven me to the back door of that very establishment on several occasions. Along with the aforementioned goods and services they sold something that resembled whiskey after hours, and on the Sabbath day as well.

"Scares me the way these gray boys take to the snow," he said, in a confidential tone. "Personally, I wouldn't touch it with a barge pole. Catch a nigger with snow he'd be lucky if they give him life in prison. Mos' likely hang him from the nearest lamp post."

I told him I didn't know why the bulls should care what people snort up their nose, or who sells it to them. It smacked of Prohibition to me. To my surprise he took exception.

"Ain't like whiskey. Folks get all jingle-brain behind it. Costs big cush, makes 'em do all kinda dirt just to get some. An' they don't bunk when they get tootin' neither. They toot some more, an' stay up all night, runnin' their mouth." He nodded at the bunch gathered around Bobby. "Lotsa these kids are tooters. It's a now an'then thing with most of'em I guess, but see that one gal? The tall, skinny one?"

He pointed out a well-dressed, nervous-looking frail standing at the edge of the crowd, gnawing her thumbnail.

"They say she's the ritz, got'er a crush on Bobby, started buyin' snow t'show him how hep she is. Now she got the habit, bad.

"There's two hope-to-die-snowbirds hang out here," he added. "The rich gal an' Wigger. Used to be three, but one of'em went down for the count awhile back."

"Snow kill him?"

"Not exactly."

As you can imagine, I've developed an ear for the sort of tale that ends in death and this one was truly strange. The kid had gotten into the habit of stepping outside and sniffing nose candy a few times per evening. Inevitably, at some point during one of those tooters, a mood would come upon him, he'd let out a blood-curdling whoop, bolt across Front Avenue, scramble over the Calvary Cemetery fence, and spend the next while tipping over gravestones.

"He'd come back all outta breath and sweaty, big grin all over his map. Me an'the band be swingin'away, and we'd hear a cheer when he walked in. 'Yay Tipper. Attaboy Tipper.' But one night, maybe a year ago, he didn't come back. Next day they found him over in the graveyard, squashed like a bug under one'a them big old monuments."

He said the stone that crushed him weighed eight hundred pounds. There was some hooch-talk about the revenge of the stiffs, but the sober surmise was that he'd gotten to rocking that monument back and forth in order to tip it over, and it tipped the wrong way.

"Rocking a piece of stone that weighs eight hundred pounds?" I was incredulous.

"Snow give a man superhuman powers," he explained. "'Specially the oxford gray. They claim they go a week without sleepin', make love twelve hours straight, go down to the pool hall an' run the table— rack'em up, do it over again—sounds kinda suspicious to me too."

"Better tell those porter friends'a yours to watch out," I advised. "White kids whiffin' snow, dyin' under suspicious circumstances .."

"Oh, the porters ain't sellin' it no more."

"Coppers on to'em?"

He shook his head no. There'd been no local pressure, he explained, but the crew chief had taken all the porters and conductors aside, one crew at a time as they passed through Chicago, and told them to quit peddling in St. Paul.

"Man said it'd cost'em their job if they done it. Trainmen think the mob got after'em. Want it all to themselves."

"No mob here," I said. "We got a different set up."

He nodded as if he knew. "Some gal's sellin' it 'round town now."

I should get out like this more often, I thought. You learn things in these joints you'll never hear at Tin Cup's.

"She come in here?" I asked.

"Uh-uh. Nobody ever sees her. Dutchy's the man here."

I was eager to hear more, but Bobby Jr. tugged on his sleeve. Bobby was about to put on a performance, and he wanted everybody's attention.

The crowd around him hushed. He closed his eyes until a scratchy recording of I'm Comin' Virginia came on the Wurlitzer, tapped his foot patiently all the way through Trumbauer's saxophone opening, then mimed that entire Bix solo, swaying and fingering an imaginary coronet right through to the long fade at the end.

"Bobby's on to somethin'," my smoke companion whispered. "Can't play a note far's I know, but he understands 'bout the music."

"Understands what?"

"The real jazz ain't about dancin,' it's about tellin' a story."

The gals stared at Bobby in rapt admiration. The guys had envy written all over their faces, not of the performance, which was so corny it was embarrassing, but of the effect it had on the gals.

I told my smoke informant my name before the band reassembled to play, and he gave me his: Sean. Sometimes I feel like the modern world is passing me by.

My eyes were accustomed to the light by then. I noticed Slapper Doran and a couple of his fighters at a table near the stage. It didn't look like they'd come to do battle with the Hun. I couldn't picture them doing the Lindy Hop either.

Bobby and Amy drifted off when the music started, and took the crowd with them. Angie stuck around. A stool opened next to her, so I sat down. I had to lean right into her ear to talk, then turn my head so she could lean into mine when she replied.

"He's quite the performer, your brother."

"That pretend horn-playin' routine? I don't know. He's got a pretty good voice though."

"Piano player just told me about kid name'a Tipper. You know about him?"

"Sure. Neighborhood guy. Friend of my brother's. Terrible what happened. He knocked a big gravestone over on himself."

Her lips lingered after she spoke, and brushed my cheek when I turned to reply. I spotted Wigger out of the corner of my eye, looking ruefully at our tete a tete. It was pretty obvious he was soft on Angie. And just as obvious that Angie was vamping me.

"Kid had a headfull'a toot," I said. "Must'a made him crazy."

"It affects people different ways." She put her hand on my leg. "Makes some feel like jazzin' it. Want a little?"

"Nah, I'm strictly a hoocher, Angie. So, they think he pushed eight hundred pounds'a granite over, and managed to wind up underneath it?"

She wondered why I was interested. Force of habit, I explained. I hear about a murder, I investigate.

"What about dad. Figured out who killed him yet?"

"I discovered who everybody thinks killed him."

"You don't think it might be somebody else, do you?"

"Just tryin' to keep an open mind."

She didn't hide her disappointment when I said I was leaving. Angie clearly expected me to pitch some woo. I rarely hesitated when a gal gave me the come-on in those days, but something, the thought of her sister maybe, gave me pause.

I tried to say goodbye to Bobby Jr. but couldn't get his attention. He was out on the dance floor, cutting it up with Amy. Bobby was a smooth hoofer. They did a break out, and Amy's dress flew up to reveal a pair of knockout gams and some pink underwear. There were catcalls and wolf whistles.

I walked past Wigger and Slapper Doran on the way out. They were huddled together, deep in discussion.

****

Next morning I called Marcie to arrange a meeting.

"Mr and Mrs. Kirkwood are vacationing in Canada for two weeks," said the maid.

I considered putting everything on hold until our next meeting, so we could meet yet again after I got back to work. That seemed inexcusable, and besides it was always a pleasure chinning with Teddy Eccles. I wanted to drop by his office. Instead, he suggested lunch at the Green Lantern a few days hence. I prefer other venues when people take me to lunch, but didn't argue.

I visited Betty Tuttweiler again the next afternoon and had a nice, pleasant, uninformative little chat. Angie wasn't home. Bobby was asleep.

When it became apparent that I was settling in to wait him out, Betty started knitting her hands again, probably out of embarrassment. When Bobby finally came down-stairs he was arm in arm with Amy.

Long engagements were common in those days due to
the Depression. That loosened the premarital sex taboo
considerably, but sleeping together in the parental abode
was still pretty daring. So was the loving couple's behavior.
Amy mumbled something about getting home. They gave
each other a farewell buss at the door that lingered, esca-
lated and threatened to turn into something best done in
private. Betty cleared her throat, they broke it off and Amy
said goodbye.

Bobby sat down to some warmed over coffee. He said
he missed his dad every day, told me he'd tried to hold the
business together after the murder but quit in frustration
when he realized most of the records had been kept in Bobby Sr.'s noggin.

"I called on all his accounts. They bought a few times
out of respect for dad, but after awhile they were askin'
questions about seasonal buying, how many blooms they
could move and when. Stuff like that." He looked over at
Betty. "Dad learned it from the ground up. I'd have to be a
delivery boy for five years to even begin—"

"Bobby, Bobby." She mussed his hair fondly. "You don't
have to sell flowers. Sell bonds. That's where the money is."

"You don't get it, ma. Old guys sell bonds to the fat cats.
Guys my age sell bonds to their relatives."

"Exactly," she said.

"You wanna buy some bonds?" He laughed. "How's
about Angie?"

"How's about the Ervines," she replied, and she raised
an eyebrow.

It was an allusion to the well-known White Bear million-aires. Sounded like a long shot to me.

Bobby just repeated the common wisdom when we moved on to the murder. "Marcie knows who bumped him off," he said. "We all do."

"So you don't think it's possible anybody else shot him?" I asked.

He shrugged, torched a fag and took a deep pull.

"Well if somebody else did, who might it have been?"

"I can't imagine," said Betty.

Neither could Bobby, apparently. He was half-hidden in smoke, off in a dream.

"Hey, Bobby. You snort snow?"

He shook his head no, slowly. "Gin's my poison,— 'Gimme a pig's foot and a bottle'a gin,'" he chanted, "'jazz me cuz I'm in my sin.'"

Now I'd heard a smoke gal singing something like that on the Wurlitzer, and Bobby's version was so self-con-sciously derivative that you'd have been tempted to laugh, except for one thing. He had the kind of growly, smoker's voice we liked in those days, and to the extent you could tell from such a short riff, maybe the gift for phrasing too.

"Why do you ask him about snow?" Betty inquired. She was working her hands a mile a minute. It was disconcert-ing.

"Just curious," I said. "I come to find out a lotta guys around Kuby's whiff snow."

"Bobby dear, you never told me that," she said.

"Don't worry, ma. I'm there for the sounds and a little

taste'a hooch, that's all."

He blew a smoke ring, sat back and began fingering that phantom horn again. It seemed Betty was used to his eccentricities. She asked what he was playing.

"Goofin'," he said. "Bix called it 'correlated phrasing.'"

"You should take trumpet lessons, darling."

"Nah." He stuck the fag in his puss and closed his eyes.

"Maybe voice ," I suggested. "You could be up on that bandstand, Bobby. Right up front."

He blushed, and continued correlating phrases.

****

Next day I met with Teddy at the Green Lantern—a joint where the clientele told you all you needed to know about our city in the thirties.

Some gawkers showed up there in the evening, and of course the inevitable retinue of frails who get their kicks hanging out with gangsters, but during the day it was it was cops and robbers about fifty-fifty—strictly a place to exchange scuttlebutt and pass messages, spoken and unspoken.

I was making an effort to put off drinking until five P M in those days so I wasn't around the Lantern much, but when I was, it was in the company of Teddy or Jack Moylan. They were both good friends, and being seen with either served my purposes. The coppers were reminded that I had a direct line to the D A's office through Teddy, which kept them, if not honest, more honest than they'd be otherwise. The gangsters, who were sometimes inconvenienced by what I discovered, took note of my familiarity with Officer Jack. They might not care much for me, but they wanted to be on good terms him.

Whichever one I was with, I made sure the maitre'd walked us through to a back booth so everybody could see. Jack and Teddy were both big men, bigger than me and I'm six feet. Jack looked like he could knock your block off with a backhand slap. Teddy had a mane of thick, prematurely gray hair, and a ready smile for all, because all were potential clients.

The Lantern had drapes over the windows, lots of tables, booths along two walls, a long bar, and some nicely subdued light from a row of chandeliers with green-tinted bulbs. It gave the impression of class, which was dispelled once you tasted the food. Teddy and I nursed beers, and pushed our Salisbury Steak around in puddles of grease while we caught up.

A little scamp of a kid wearing patched pants and a worker's cap stuck a bouquet of roses in my face. I declined. Teddy bought one, gave him a buck and told him to keep the change.

Harry Sawyer, owner and proprietor, was seated in a booth along the far wall. He was in a heated conversation with Faennis Cuhulain, a man who seemed too gentlemanly to be what he was, a refugee from the Chicago gang wars. Capone had murdered his buddy Dion O'Banion, aka Gimpy, who'd run that city's North Side syndicate out of his flower shop.

Cuhulain was an oddity at the Lantern, neither a copper nor a wanted man. Rumor had it he'd simply been told to leave Chicago if he valued his life. Apparently he did, and the way he lived you could see why. He was fiftyish, a snazzy dresser, and said to be a connoisseur of food, music and other pleasures. He kept a suite of rooms at the St. Paul Hotel.

I had a notion of what Sawyer and Cuhulain's discussion concerned. Sawyer had inherited the Lantern and the sinecure it represented from his ex-boss Dan Hogan, who'd devised the layover system and made it work. According to the terms of the original layover a wanted criminal could come to St. Paul and live for up to a year under police protection, as long as he paid Hogan five thousand clams (it was a sliding scale; that was minimum) and committed no crimes in the immediate area. Hogan split the gratuity with the coppers, and his gang made sure the mugs behaved. It was a system that worked nicely as long as Hogan lived.

No one knew for sure who'd wired Hogan's bucket, but Sawyer certainly prospered after it blew up. Sawyer had no interest in disciplining gangsters. He preferred acting as their banker, and lately he'd been doing so in cahoots with Cuhulain. At least that was the rumor. I neither knew if it was true, nor cared. I'd been banking with Sawyer since the 1930 bank run, but it was the other side of that coin that really affected my life, and much for the better. After Sawyer went into financial services Eternal Tommy had to reach into the ranks and find someone to enforce the terms of the layover. My friend Jack Moylan was his choice.

"How's things," Teddy asked. "How's Jerk doing?"

"I don't see much of him nowadays."

"Why's that?"

"He double-crossed me."

I told him about the Margaret Thornton affair. Teddy said it didn't qualify as a double-cross, just a devious way of looking out for my best interests.

"That's one way of lookin' at it."

"Jesus, Martin. He's family."

"Which means of all people, he should know better."

"Know better than what?"

"Than to deke me into stepping out of character. Jesus, I get steamed just thinkin' about it! I felt like an organ-grinder's monkey. And here Jerk knew who was behind it the whole time."

"Did you learn anything?"

That was always Teddy's question. He was philosophically committed to the idea that no experience was wasted, because life was series of lessons about the human condition. It was a good enough theory that we chewed it over on many a drunken evening, during which, as I recall, I argued that life was just getting from one end to the other without tripping over your dick— but who knows?

"I heard some good music," I admitted.

"There you go.—So, what is it you wanted to discuss?"

I told him what I knew about the Tuttweiler case, and asked why the D A wouldn't try to nail Sheldon Slansky on motive and opportunity.

"Good question, but I've got a better one. How come that's all he's got?"

"Eddy claims he couldn't crack the guy's alibi, couldn't find the weapon, couldn't get any evidence at all. My client thinks he wasn't lookin' hard enough because some of the insurance money ended up in his pocket."

"I'm the DA, I'm going to check that out," said Teddy. "Unless the rest of it ended up in my pocket."

"Think that might've happened?"

"Martin, in a world where enlightened self-interest is the guiding principle we can never discount that possibility. Who's the client?"

He whistled when I told him. Turned out he knew her because he'd defended her husband.

"You probably remember," he said. "It was front page news. 'White Bear Youth In Sports Car Collision. Negligence Alleged.' That was Dirk Kirkwood. He was remorseful, I'll say that for him. He should've been. Him and his buddies used to get lit at the Yacht Club, and race their sports cars on the county roads out there. He was trying to pass another kid's Stutz in some kind of English roller skate when he sideswiped a horse and wagon. Dirk was barely scratched, but he killed the poor bastard in the wagon."

"He was lucky."

"Drunk. That helps. Keeps you loose while you're flying fifty feet into a swamp. We settled out of court for a pretty penny after the charges were dropped."

"Him and Marcie married then?"

"No. I went to their wedding a few months later. I suppose I must've met her father, don't remember. I remember her though. There was talk that Dirk was marrying down, and I wondered why. One look at the bride solved that mystery. She still a lulu?"

Must've been a certain expression on my mug when I nodded.

"I don't mind helping you out professionally Martin, but you're on your own when it comes to pokin' clients." He consulted his watch. "I have to run. You'll hear from me."

I watched him make his slow way out, pausing several times on the way to chat. He stopped at Sawyer's table, slapped Faennis Cuhulain on the back, and told a joke that left the two of them laughing. He waved when he reached the door, I raised my hand to wave back, and the waiter noticed.

That's how I found out lunch was on me.

****

A few nights later I heard the din of angry voices as I walked into Tin Cup's. A crowd of neighborhood guys had Little Mikey Bailey the beat copper surrounded. They were shouting threats. I spotted Billy Powell and Tim McKenna among them. Neither were particularly pugnacious fellows, but they looked grim.

"What's goin' on?" I asked McKenna.

He could barely contain his outrage long enough to explain. Then, just as he began, in walked Eddy Guilfoyle. The mob gathered around him, and started dishing out the same abuse only louder.

Eddy still looked awful, but being forced to defend himself acted as a tonic. He put his big nose right in their faces. Soon he'd shouted them down.

"That Kraut and the poison he was peddlin' corrupted the youth of our parish!" he said, when they'd quieted enough to hear him.

"Ya made a rat outta Slapper Doran," said someone in the crowd.

"That young man made a rat of himself," was Guilfoyle's rejoinder, "and if he rats under oath he might stay out of prison, which is more than he deserves.—G'wan, the lot'a yez!"

He pushed his way through to the bar. No one tried to stop him.

"Whiskey," he said. "And one for Little Mikey."

Mikey squirmed in beside him.

I didn't have the temerity to ask Eddy what it was all about, but Tim filled me in. Word had gone around that little Mikey had collared Slapper Doran at Eddy's behest, frisked him, and found a quantity of nose candy in his pocket. Then Eddy put the squeeze on Slap, and forced him to introduce an undercover bull to the Kraut he'd been buying the stuff from over at Kuby's.

"He got the Hun to sell some to the copper," said Tim. "Now the Hun's in the hoosegow, and Slap's gonna testify against him when he goes to trial to save his own bacon."

Tim didn't know the seller's name, but little Mikey confirmed my suspicions later that evening. It was Angie's friend, Wigger.

The list of things that I don't believe in is longer than a whore's dream, and coincidence is right there at the top— flower peddlers, nose candy, Eddy G and his mysterious lack of progress; they all fit together somehow, and the way I saw it, they had to be connected to Bobby Tuttweiler's murder.

I tried to approach Eddy about it. "I don't ever want to hear about that case again," he said, "ok?"

That was too bad, but it could have been worse. Eddy would get over it and meanwhile, each new twist was an opportunity for another meeting with Marcie. I was slowly pondering how to proceed a few days later when Teddy called.

"Find out where the insurance settlement went," he said. "I tried. All I could find out was where it didn't go, and that was interesting. It didn't go to bribe the D A, I can guarantee you that, and I'm ninety-nine percent sure it didn't go to Eddy Guilfoyle. Make that ninety-nine point nine. And the suspect doesn't have it either. So where is it?"

Teddy said the D A's office would have been glad to charge Slansky with the murder if they could've shown he'd profited by it, but they'd discovered the opposite.

"He's living like a church mouse," Teddy said. "His business is closed. His bank account is empty. He referees softball games for a living, if you can call that a living. They've been over his finances with a fine-toothed comb. The man has nothing. As far as they can tell he didn't even pay the lawyer who pressured the insurance company for him. Somebody else did."

"Who?"

"Well, that's good question. Attorney's name is Morris Fischbein, but I know Morrie. You'll never get anything out of him. The D A tried. He just said it was none of their business."

"So the D A's office doesn't have a clue where the money went?"

"Yeah, they have a clue, and a theory to go with it. Bobby Tuttweiler was a come-easy-go-easy type of guy, didn't have a pot to piss in when he died, but the widow is doing just fine near as anyone can tell. They think maybe the suspect gave the cash to the widow."

"Why?"

To prove to her at least that he didn't kill her husband in order to collect on that policy."

"Twenty grand? The whole thing?"

"Sounds excessive to me too, my friend, but it's the best anyone can come up with.—Thanks for lunch by the way."

"My pleasure."

"Let me know what happens," said Teddy. "I find it pretty interesting."

I found it interesting too, so much so that curiosity drove me out of Tin Cup's and over to Dunning Field for the Wednesday evening softball games.

There were five in progress. It was a regular league— uniforms, umps, the works. Slansky was easy to spot. He was a squared off fire plug of a guy, with the regulation Hebe beezer, and big sad eyes. The other umps yelled STEEE- RIKE! He just raised his arm and muttered, "strike."

I stood behind the backstop and watched from his perspective for awhile.

This was a few years before the advent of the Kitten Ball, which is so big it takes two hands to catch, and so light no mitt is required. A Kittenball game is mostly about lobbing the ball to the batter, who whacks it with all his might. The best players are middle-aged lunks who hit the thing so far that they can haul their beer bellies around the bases on their stiff old legs before the ball can be thrown back to the infield.

Softball, on the other hand, is an athletic contest, and I enjoyed watching it that evening. The pitchers whirled their arms around like aeroplane propellers three or four times before letting fly underhand. The ball—which, name notwithstanding, is not soft—came zooming in as fast as any major league pitcher could throw, that was how it looked to me. It took a brave batsman to stand in there and swing, but when they connected it went a long way.

A couple times foul tips almost beaned Slansky, but he pulled his head back between his shoulders just barely enough to avoid getting clunked. He reminded me of a turtle.

"Who'ya like in the series?" I asked him, between innings.

"Tigers," he replied, without bothering to turn around.

It figured. The Tigers first baseman was Hank Greenberg, the only Mocky in the game to my knowledge. The Tigers had won the series the year before, but Greenberg broke his wrist in game two, so it was a bittersweet victory for the people of the book.

I'd played enough sandlot ball to appreciate the finer points of the game, and liked to think of myself as above such considerations, but truth is I'd never warmed up to

Babe Ruth, who'd retired the year before, or the Yanks generally. They were a team that featured Huns and Wops.

Which team you cheered for, I might add, was the least of the ethnic bias in St. Paul. A few years later, on Halloween Night, there was a radio drama on the air featuring fake news bulletins of Martians invading earth. The hysteria it caused is hard to imagine if you weren't there. People were piling into flivers and streaming out of town by the thousands, which, on our end of the city, meant heading through St. Albert's parish. I sat it out at Tin Cup's, preferring death at the hands of bug-eyed monsters to life without a drink. Later, when the refugees began straggling back, I heard that Rice Street had been lined with Krauts brandishing baseball bats, not to fight off the Martians, but to prevent something worse, Micks driving through their neighborhood unmolested.

After the games were over the players and umps gathered on the Central High School side of the field and drank beer. Slansky didn't join them. He plodded over to the sidelines on his thick legs and began slowly gathering up equipment. The sun was low and the heat of the day had eased. I watched him for awhile.

"You Sheldon Slansky," I said.

"Yes," he replied, quietly. "And you're a cop."

I assured him I wasn't but offered no further explanation. Nor did he ask for one.

"You're here to talk about Bobby Tuttweiler, whoever you are. I've been dealing with this long enough I can tell. I didn't kill him. Any other questions?"

"Yeah, what'd you do with the insurance money?"

"Oh, you're from the D A's office."

"Nope. I've been hired to find out who killed Bobby. If the D A won't charge you, that's good enough for me. I'd just like your help finding out who did."

He shook his head, as if to ask what kind of chump I thought he was. I could see his point.

"I'm in your shoes I wouldn't trust me either, but look at it this way. If I'm successful, the burden's off'a you."

He mulled that over long enough so I half expected him to start talking.

"You don't understand," he finally said. "You couldn't. I've been in the middle of it for a year and I don't understand. Who hired you?"

"Can't tell'ya. It's unethical."

"Nice talking to you."

He turned his back, stuffed a catcher's mask into a big canvas bag, and started picking up odds and ends—a bag of resin, a rule book. He went about it methodically, one thing at a time. I watched him for awhile then cleared my throat.

"You still here," he said.

"Gonna give me anything if I tell you who's my client?"

"I won't if you don't. We'll see otherwise."

I told him. It seemed to sink in.

"Marcella," he said. "I barely remember her. She was married by the time she was 18. Some rich kid."

He paused, scratched his head. A little smile inched across his puss, the first emotion I'd seen him show. After a bit he started talking again.

"Good thing Marcella left home when she did. Otherwise I'd have had to hire her too. The rest of Bobby's family was on my payroll at one time or another. Bobby always complained I didn't pay him enough, but as far as I was concerned every nickel I paid them was money he cost me. I had Betty making bouquets and wreaths out in front of the shop for awhile. She knew from nothing about flower arranging, but she wasn't a total write-off. There aren't many men in the retail flower business any more, but the few there were came around and bought from me, so they could try to get in her pants. Y'see, word got around that if you approached Betty at the right time, she might say yes. Problem was, she didn't just go have a quickie. She made a big production out of it, disappeared for a few days, wrecked homes. It was bad for business."

He shook his head as if he were remembering something painful, but he still had that little smile.

"Angie and Bobby Jr.? They were a complete waste of money. Angie was supposed to handle walk-ins. Showed up about half the time, and bitched if I didn't pay her for the days she missed. I tried Bobby Jr. in sales. Good looking kid, but he had his head in the clouds. Drew a salary for a year and never sold much."

"So why'd you hire'em?"

"Because Bobby wanted me to and I couldn't risk losing him, that's why. Bobby Tuttweiler was the kind who comes along once in a lifetime, if you're lucky. There'll never be another guy who can sell flowers like he did.—I also paid for a room he kept at the St. Paul Hotel. Told me he used it 'for business purposes' (now he grinned for real). You're not supposed to mix business with pleasure, but Bobby was the exception who proves that rule... Anyway, it's different now, that's for sure. He took all my accounts with him when he left, and then it got split up between three four wholesalers after he was murdered. Makes no difference to me. I went bankrupt. Had it all to myself for years, now I have nothing and everybody thinks I killed him. But damn it, I did not kill Bobby Tuttweiler."

"Must'a given it some thought. I would, if I lost everything. Eddy Guilfoyle said you were threatening him."

"That's a lie. You know Guilfoyle?"

"I know every bull in town," I said, in the ominous tone I use when I tell people that.

"He's quite the ladies man," Slansky said.

"Uhh, no. Not Eddy."

"Really? I thought he was a regular Rudolph Valentino. He slept with one of the most beautiful women I ever laid eyes on."

"We're thinkin' of two different people," I told him. "The Eddy Guilfoyle I know looks like Paddy's pig, and he's been happily married twenty five years to a woman who could pass for Fatty Arbuckle if she tucked her hair under her hat."

"That's him. Eddy Guilfoyle. Betty Tuttweiler found him irresistible. Must be that nose of his."

This was either a flat lie or the most interesting fact I'd unearthed since the key man policy.

"You certain?" I asked.

"Yeah."

"I don't believe it. How do you know?"

"My attorney told me."

"And how does he know?"

"It's his business to know things like that. After Bobby was murdered I went to somebody you've probably heard of, Leon Gleeman. Told him I needed help. He put me in touch with his own lawyer. 'Don't worry,' Leon told me, 'Morrie'll take care of it.' And he did."

That was certainly plausible. Gleeman had a better pipeline to the buzz than I did.

"Well, for arguments sake, let's assume Eddy did sleep with Betty Tuttweiler," I said. "What's the difference?"

"Betty and Bobby wanted me to drop the key man policy and I refused. When Bobby was murdered, Betty told Guilfoyle about it, and he came after me. He couldn't find any evidence, because there isn't any. I didn't do it, but she kept him comin' after me. Any way she could."

"You have to admit you were a good suspect."

"Doesn't mean he shouldn't look for anyone else, but he never did. My lawyer thinks Betty wanted to use his investigation as the basis for a civil suit, so she could get that insurance money. He figured she planned to sue for unjust enrichment."

"So why didn't she?"

"Maybe because she found out I didn't have the money. Also, she knows in her heart that I didn't kill Bobby. We go back a long way, Betty and me. She knows damn well I never could've shot Bobby. Truth is, I liked the guy. Everybody did."

"Not everybody.—If you didn't shoot him, who did?"

"I wish I knew." He pulled the cords tight on the canvas bag, and carefully tied a square knot.

He concentrates on details because the big picture doesn't bear looking at, that was how it seemed to me.

The long springtime dusk had begun while we were talking. The electric lights on Marshall Avenue hadn't come on yet, but the gas lamps on the nearby side streets were lit. Laughter and a few scraps of conversation drifted over from the other side of the field. I knew Slansky wanted to be over there with them, talking baseball, drinking beer. But he couldn't. It would've been hard enough just because he was a Hebe, but everybody thought he was a murderer too. That made it impossible.

"How's this," I said. "You tell me where the money went, I'll find out who killed him."

"If I tell you where the money went, I won't live to hear about it."

"Really? That sounds promising."

"What, the lead, or I won't live? Get me killed and the whole thing goes away. Shelly shot Bobby, somebody shot Shelly. Case closed."

"I'm not kiddin'. If the kinda mugs who kill people are connected to the money, I know I'm on the right track."

"That doesn't solve my problem. I'm the only person can tell you where the money went, and the man I gave it to knows that."

"Maybe he killed Bobby."

"I doubt it. They were friends, and besides, Bobby was

worth more to him alive. Me, I'm worth nothing to him. Not now."

"But what were you worth in the first place? Why'd you take that policy out and keep on payin' while you were goin' bust?"

"Easy now.—You're asking the right questions, but you're way ahead of yourself.—I told you he'd kill me if he found out, and if you talk to him he'll know. There's no way around it."

"There wouldn't be if he stuck the money under his pillow. But if he used it and you tell me how, then I could claim I worked backwards and found out."

He thought that over for awhile.

"Why should I trust you?" he asked.

"My client and me, we're interested in the truth. Nobody else seems to be. We're your only hope."

He thought it over for awhile, sighed, and said, "He's one of your people. Name's Faennis Cuhulain. If I had to guess, I'd say he used it the same way I would've. He bought flowers.—Oh, and I kept the policy as an enticement. Told Bobby if he came back to work for me, the proceeds were his when he retired."

He threw the canvas bag over his shoulder and plodded off into the gathering darkness before I could ask him anything else. Didn't matter. What I'd learned constituted such a great stride forward that I decided to take a few days off. I wanted to meet with Marcie again before proceeding, and besides, I had to think things through. I needed to approach Cuhulain, but there was no obvious way to do it.

Officer Jack would be no help. Cuhulain didn't need anyone's protection as long as he stayed out of Chicago, and that was the least of it. Capone, who'd murdered Cuhulain's pal O'Banion, and several hundred other rivals, decided to make a deal with Cuhulain. Nobody knew the particulars, but he was a survivor and there was an air about him—part danger, part sophistication. Best be careful, that was my attitude.

I decided to call Teddy again. I told him my investigation had taken an interesting turn and asked if he could arrange a meeting with Cuhulain. That really piqued his interest, but I kept my trap shut about the reason. He asked if he could sit in. I agreed. Then I made the usual arrangement with Marcie.

****

The afternoon crowd at the Criterion was getting used to us. I suppose they filled in the blanks with lurid speculation. I could feel their eyes follow me to a back booth, and of course heads swivelled a few minutes later when Marcie walked in. She was sporting a golden tan, and wearing a sleeveless dress cut low enough so her pince nez rested on sun-kissed flesh.

She told me that she and The Lucky Dog had been to some island in Lake Michigan.

"I relaxed for awhile, but by the time a week went by your, um— investigation was on my mind again," she said. "So what've you found out?"

I told her that nobody, including me, liked Slansky for the murder. That didn't please her at all.

"Has somebody got a better idea?" she asked. "He takes out a life insurance policy on my dad, keeps payin' it after my dad quits on him, even though his business is practically busted, then collects double the face amount because my dad is murdered? That's some coincidence."

"I hear'ya, but according to the D A he doesn't have the money."

"Maybe he spent it." she said.

"If so, there's no trace of how. It's hard to spend twenty grand without leaving a trail of some kind."

"Not if you're a florist. Florists buy flowers with cash. I learned a few things growin' up with my dad.—More than a few."

"I suppose it's possible he bought flowers. I'll check into it. The D A thinks he gave that money to somebody."

"Well?" she demanded, leaning over the table, looking irritated—"who?"—The specs swung loose from her bosom. I averted my eyes.

"I can tell you one theory they're considering," I said. "Maybe it went to your mother."

"Who said that? I'll slap his mug, whoever it was."

"Easy. Want a drink?"

"NO!" She drummed her manicured nails on the table.

"Yes." She waved at the waiter, and ordered a Manhattan.

She calmed down after a few sips. I could tell she was getting ready to ask about my plan, which would require a reply. Which would move our meeting toward a conclusion.

"Tell me about buyin' twenty grand worth'a flowers," I said.

"You should go to someone who knows what they're talkin' about. What I can tell you is obvious. Florists buy as many flowers as they can sell before they go stale. Their price per bloom goes down as the volume goes up."

"Twenty large. That's a lotta posies."

She didn't respond immediately. I sloshed my whiskey and water around, watched her take a few more tentative sips, then guzzle her Manhattan.

"Another?" I asked. She nodded curtly, but in the affirmative.

"I once heard my dad explain the flower business to some rich men," she said, after the waiter brought her drink. "In one sentence."

"Remember it?"

"Sure. 'Men like to buy flowers from dames, and dames like to buy flowers from me.' Somethin' about the way they laughed made me feel funny, but I didn't know what. I was only fourteen. A few years later I understood. They knew his reputation, and he was bragging. They were impressed, can you imagine?"

"Yeah."

"I suppose you'd have laughed too."

I dodged that one, wisely, judging from her tone as she continued.

"My father-in-law was one of'em. What do you think of that, Martin? Come on, I want to hear if you know anything about *corruption*. Maybe you're not the man for this job."

"My, aren't we in a lousy mood.—Where were you and your father when this happened?"

"On a golf course. Probably the one we belong to now, the Dellwood Country Club. I didn't notice. I was too young to be wowed by that kinda thing back then. Now I'm too jaded. I went from too young to too jaded with hardly any in between time when I could, y'know—*revel*."

I liked the sound of that word, the way she said it. I'd had drinks with women in this state of mind before, and knew the possibilities—tears, flying glasses, sudden passionate kisses. She was well into that second Manhattan. I tried to think of a nice neutral question.

"Your father took'ya golfin' often, did he?"

"No, matter of fact that was the only time. He was talkin' with those men about some money for Midland Florists, but he always had a couple schemes in mind."

"Yeah?"

She sniffed back what might have been a tear, or the bourbon stinging her nose. Her eyes were kind of shiny, which certainly didn't detract from her appeal.

"'Yeah,' Martin. They were there to discuss money, but the other men were bringin' their sons along, so dad figured he might as well bring his daughter and see if anything came of it."

I didn't take her meaning for a moment.

"Ah. He wanted to see if their sons had any interest in his daughter."

She nodded, and took another gulp.

"Well, so? One of'em did."

"Oh, they all did. At least Dirk wasn't tacky about it. There anything wrong with that, Martin? Is it, oh, I don't know—*corrupt*?"

I sensed I was on thin ice, but forged ahead anyway.

"You've got a good marriage. That's what you told me, remember."

"Yeah."

"Yeah you remember, or yeah you've got a good marriage?"

"Both." Her eyes narrowed. "What's your point?"

"So, you used animal magnetism to get what you want. Nothin' wrong with that."

"Gallant of'ya to say so, Martin." She raised her glass. "Here's to animal magnetism. And usin' it."

I touched her glass, tentatively, ready to put my free hand in front of my face, but she just drained it and raised her hand for the waiter.

"Think maybe you've had enough?" I asked.

"Put it on the bill."

"That's not what I'm talkin' about."

She didn't respond, but after the waiter brought her drink she spoke more softly.

"I liked Dirk when I was in high school, but I never would've married him if it wasn't for an accident he had. A man was killed. Before that he was silly, but that accident changed him. I couldn't say exactly how, but he was different enough so I could marry him and get out of our house. That's the main reason I care for him to this day. Because he got me out. I was sick of it."

Suddenly she was crying. The waiter walked over and handed her a cloth napkin.

Pretty soon she'd composed herself enough to get into that Manhattan again, a worrisome development in itself.

"You ok?" I asked.

She teared up again, quietly this time.

"This is weighin' on me, Martin. Does my mother have that money?"

Her voice, her eyes, everything about her, was pleading with me to say no, which of course I did.

"How d'you know?" she sniffled.

"Because I know who Slansky gave it to."

"Who? Tell me." She wiped her eyes and took a sip of her drink.

"Uh-uh. Not yet. I'm gonna talk to him first and get to the bottom of this thing, like'ya hired me to do."

She didn't insist. She seemed calmer on the surface, but I could tell her mind was still churning. I tried to think of something to get her off track.

"When I was a kid we had a priest talked to us about corruption of the flesh and the promise of life eternal," I said. "He told us we'd wake up some morning, look in the mirror and realize we were corrupt too.—The Church, that's where you got this corruption thing on your mind."

She looked at me quizzically. "I hardly remember the Church. This is real."

"So's this," I said, pointing at my mug. "I earned these lines. Pretty soon they'll be honest to god wrinkles. We're all corrupt."

Her eyes crinkled. "You're still a good looking man," she said.

That didn't exactly address the issue, but I was flattered. I also thought things were pretty well defused at that point.

"And you're not a phony either, Martin," she continued. "That's what real *corruption* is. Those bankers friends of my father-in-law's with their one-track minds; all those gangsters that hide in St. Paul; Dirk and his—his silly drinking buddies. None of'em are saints, far from it, but they aren't hip—hip—"

"Hypocrites?"

"Kerrr—rect, and that's what Lt. Eddy Guilfoyle is. A hypocrite. He pretends to be a policeman. He should be ashamed to put a uniform on."

"He doesn't," I said. "He's a plainclothesman."

It seemed like a reasonable observation, but she glared when she heard it. "Screw you," she muttered.

She finished her Manhattan, then closed her eyes and shivered the way you do when the hooch catches up all of a sudden.

"No, screw me," she said louder, loud enough so a couple guys at a nearby table heard it. "C'mon, less go." She stood abruptly and wobbled in place for a moment.

"We're off to a hotel," she told the guys, in a confidential tone. "Martin n'me."

Their jaws dropped. She smiled a crooked smile. "C'mon, Martin. Whatter—whatter you... waitin'—."

"Uh, the bill—"

"Bills, bills, bills" she sorted through her purse, pulled out a handful of ones and dropped them on the table. "C'mon.—Wait!"

Slowly, still leaning against the booth, she crooked one long gam at the knee, and plucked off a high-heeled sandal.

Her skirt hiked up her thigh in the process, revealing the snaps that fastened her silk stockings to her garters, which were situated above the tan line, well into the alabaster zone.

"Don't wanna fall," she confided with a wink to her audience, which by then had grown to include everyone in the place.

She did the same with the other leg. When she'd finally secured both sandals in one hand, and her purse in the other, I took her by the arm and walked her out the door.

The heat was staggering. The sun was blinding. Marcie began to hiccup.

"Where's your—HIC—your aut—auto-mo -

"Right down here," I said.

A girl standing on the corner with an armful of roses spotted us and came running over. I tried to brush her off but Marcie insisted on buying the whole bouquet, and handed over a sawbuck. That little gal must've thought she'd died and gone to heaven. She followed us down University Avenue uttering thank yous, then held the door of the bucket while I stuffed Marcie in, roses and all.

"I don't wanna—HIC—go to the St. Francis," she said. "Less'go to the—HIC—Sain'paul Ho—Hotel. Ok—Martin?"

With that, she slumped back, dropped the roses on her lap, and passed out.

I should've known. That's how my luck ran with classy dames. It crossed my mind to go ahead with it anyway. I knew I wouldn't, but I drove around awhile pretending that I might. She hiccuped a few times, and mumbled something.

I considered taking her to her mother's house. That didn't sit well somehow. I wondered how she got to the Criterion. Did she drive? Did a chauffeur bring her? Eventually I settled on taking her home, wherever that was, and headed in the general direction of White Bear Lake.

By then I'd looped back to Rice Street on pure instinct, so I decided to take it north as far as I could.

I looked at her sprawled all over the seat. Marcie was a little weird, but something real was driving her nuts and she was determined to track it down. More precisely, she was determined to make me track it down. I liked that about her.

Once we passed Larpenteur Avenue blocks of neat little bungalows gave way to newly planted farm fields and acres of cow pasture. Rice Street petered out into a nameless, bumpy, gravel road. I was hoping Marcie would rouse herself and give me directions.

She finally did wake up momentarily, when we banged over a particularly jarring stretch. "O god my head," she moaned. "Turn that off." She gestured weakly toward the sun.

Roses tumbled to the floorboard. She put a hand over her eyes, leaned against the door and was out like a light again before I could say a word.

If I stay on this road I can't get lost, I reasoned, but I knew White Bear Lake lay to the east. We came to several unmarked crossroads where I could've turned, but thought better of it. Instead I squinted against the sun, which was nearing the horizon, and pressed on. The air had cooled a bit. The smell of freshly turned earth mingling with the scent of roses was pleasant enough, once my nose got over the initial shock.

I could've just driven aimlessly awhile, but soon I felt a prod from a stockinged foot. She was out the door the moment I stopped. A few roses tumbled into the ditch with her.

Some cows standing by a fence at the side of the road watched while she threw up.

"Oh shit oh dear," she muttered.

She stayed there with the dry heaves for several minutes. Eventually she steadied herself against the fence, and patted one of the cows on the nose. It mooed sympathetically.

"Where are we?" she asked.

"I was hopin' you might know."

"Oh god I feel awful... You tryin' to find my house?"

"Yeah, I didn't know what else -"

"You're a sweet guy, Martin.—Here, gimme your hand."

I reached out and helper her in. "My head," she moaned again, as she stepped up on the running board.

She closed her eyes as soon as she sat down. I thought she was out, but eventually, without opening them, she told me she lived on Birchwood Lane, on the south shore. A few minutes later I came upon a beer joint, right there in the middle of nowhere.

The bar man gave me directions, whilst a few rustics in denim overalls looked at me like I'd just arrived from Mars.

It was dusk when we entered the circle driveway in front of the Kirkwood mansion, and stopped at a cobbled walk that bisected the vast lawn up to the front steps. Marcie grabbed her shoes, a few roses, and exited, leaving the car door open behind her. She traipsed past a fellow who was watering the grass, acknowledging him en route with a slight wave of the shoes. He nodded with an amused look on his face, and watched as she stumbled up the steps to the door.

He was a handsome fellow, one of those black-haired limeys with a permanent five o'clock shadow. He was barefoot, wearing knee length striped bathing tights, and a bathing shirt. After she'd made her way inside, he walked over, leaned into the bucket and extended a hand.

"Dirk Kirkwood," he said.

"Martin McDonough."

He gave me the once-over, thorough but not unfriendly. "Had a few nips, has she?"

"You noticed."

He chuckled. "This thing with her father's murder has her pretty well flummoxed. Sure hope you can get to the bottom of it."

"I'm makin' headway," I assured him.

"Good, good. Must admit I was taken back when Marcie told me your fee, but she said you're a fellow who gets results. 'Then tell him to go to it,' I told her. It's brought up all sorts of unpleasant memories, made her quite unhappy.... So, how do you manage it?"

"Manage what?"

"To solve all those crimes."

I was relieved. I thought he meant how do you manage to get my wife drunk and try to put the make on her under the guise of professional inquiry?—Marcie had left the door to the house wide open. Faint sounds of wretching came from within. It was time to leave.

"You hafta know who to ask," I replied. "And what to ask'em." I put the floor shift in first, and slowly released the clutch.

"Fascinating. Take care old sport."

"You too."

He picked up his hose and sprayed his way back toward the Kirkwood manse. I navigated the long driveway on to Birchwood Lane, and headed for the city.

Motive and Opportunity

It was a beautiful Sunday morning in June, the kind that makes you glad to be alive even if you're hungover. I showered, dressed and made for the fliver, but Mrs. Dunn collared me at the door and browbeat me into admitting that I wasn't heading for Mass.

"Your immortal soul is in jeopardy, Martin," she clucked. "Have some breakfast, so's you don't start your shenanigans with an empty belly."

My plan had been to jump in the bucket, park downtown, grab a cup of coffee at the Town Talk, and take the trolley to Lexington Park. Teddy Eccles had arranged a nice venue for our meeting with Faennis Cuhulain; seats directly behind first base to watch the St. Paul Saints play the Minneapolis Millers.—Could I pause long enough to eat and make it for the first pitch?—Yes, if I took the Rice Street trolley and transferred at University. I followed Mrs. Dunn back down the hall and seated myself at the boarding house table.

Next to me sat the laconic Arthur O'Malley, a man several years older than myself and more confirmed in his bachelorhood. He had his nose in the Sunday comics. "Mind if I look at the sport's page," I asked.

He grunted something I took as affirmative, and almost missed his mouth with a spoonful of Mrs. Dunn's gruel, so engrossed was he in the goings on in Gasoline Alley.

The headline was startling: Schmeling KOs Brown Bomber In 12th!

I could hardly believe my eyes. I'd followed Joe Louis's career with interest, despite the melodrama the man inspired. Some sportswriter had actually written that he was, "a credit to his race—the human race." That's a tough read with your stomach in the condition mine normally is when I pick up the morning paper, but I'd absorbed the blow gamely and kept up with Louis's amazing record all that previous year. He'd fought thirteen times, and won them all.

His signature victory had come when he knocked out the former Heavyweight Champ, Primo Carnera. That didn't impress me. I'd always thought the 265 pound Carnera was a big stiff, but when Louis KOed another former champ, Maxie Baer, I was convinced. Baer had an iron jaw. I braced myself against the inevitable hyperbole, and read the tale of Louis's surprising defeat:

"The Dark Uhlan almost knocked out Louis in the fourth when he left his feet to deliver 192 pounds of dynamite on the Brown Bomber's jaw.... The Teuton's right eye was closed by the seventh, after absorbing jab after piston-like jab delivered by the meteoric negro, but the gritty German squinted and kept to his task... A right flush on the chin rocked Louis from head to heel as he came from his corner in the ninth. A glassy stare came to the negro's eyes. He staggered as if drunken but kept his feet. Another right sent him spinning..."

I couldn't finish. It was a TKO. Before I threw in the towel I took a peek at the end, by which time, "the Hun's mighty right fist was cocked with a patience known only to his Germanic countrymen as the bell tolled for the twelfth."

I grabbed the front section out from under O'Malley's nose.

Schmeling's countrymen seemed to be losing their legendary patience with the French, who'd been hoping against hope that their craven yielding of the Ruhr Valley coal mines would mollify the gritty Teutons. Fat chance.

I glanced around the table, where the likes of Frank Mullen, Robert Fogarty, and other men of draft age were polishing off their victuals so they could make eleven o'clock Mass.

"Pray for peace," I advised Mullen. "If y'want peace work'fr justice," he replied. "I do work for justice," I told him. "And what're y'workin' on now?" he inquired. "I think of it as the case of The Key Man," I surprised myself by saying, because I'd been referring to it mentally as the case of seeing how many times I could meet with Marcie. "You'll have to tell me about it one'a these days," said Mullen. "Not until I've solved the mystery," I told him, "and even then you'll need to ply me with drink." He assured me he would.

Another item in the paper was of some interest, in view of my pending engagement:

"Al Capone Stabbed By Convict—Al Capone was stabbed in the back with a scissors by a desperate fellow convict in Alcatraz prison yesterday, but the former Chicago gang overlord smashed his assailant with his fist and walked to the prison hospital. Ill feeling has been reported between Capone and other convicts since the mutiny of prisoners last January. The assailant, a leader in that fruitless movement, had been bitter against Capone because the latter refused to participate."

I could well imagine why he refused. Unlike many other inmates, Capone would be getting out soon if he behaved. He was doing a few years for tax evasion, of all things. According to my copper friends that was the G's new strategy. They planned to put every gangster in America in stir for filing false tax returns. The gangsters weren't exactly shaking in their boots at the prospect. A couple years on the rock was better than a date with Old Sparky, and implicit in the tax strategy was the admission that efforts to nail them for murder and other major felonies hadn't panned out.

I had to run half a block to catch the streetcar, which was full of people heading for Lexington Park. Newsies were hawking special editions of the Dispatch when we got off to transfer at Rice and University.

"STEADY LOU FETTE HURLIN' FOR THE SAINTS," they shouted. "GIT'CHER GAME DAY SPECIAL!"

There was a line of trolleys at the traffic light, and a big crowd queuing to get on. As soon as one streetcar filled, another crossed the intersection. "I NEED TICKETS," shouted a scalper. "I GOT TICKETS," shouted another. "GET YOUR TICKETS HERE!"

The buzz in the crowd was about two major league scouts rumored to be attending. "They're lookin' Fette over," a fellow Saints fan confided, as we boarded for the park.

This wasn't exactly good news for the home team, but I viewed Fette's ascension to the majors as inevitable. He was a big righthander who rarely yielded a walk, and threw as hard in the late innings as he did in the early ones. He was going for win number thirteen that afternoon, and the season wasn't half over.

The trolley was full by the time I got aboard. All the windows were open but it was hot nevertheless. I edged and shoved my way back to the open smoking area in the rear. It was cooler there, but not much. The car was moving so slowly that little breeze was generated. I leaned out and looked at an endless jam of flivers, trolleys, and horse and wagon rigs, including many a horse pulling an automobile for lack of gas money.

"We gonna make the first inning?" I queried my fellow passengers. "I dunno," said one. "I'm gonna get out an' walk pretty soon," said another. "Think they'll sell out?"

"Nahh," I replied. "They always squeeze in a few more."

The streetcar began to empty as it became apparent that a determined fan in need of a ticket, and unwilling to pay the scalper's premium, could walk faster. Untroubled by such mundane concerns, I seated myself and rode until we came to a complete halt a few blocks east of Lexington

Avenue. Then I made my leisurely way to the Will Call window, where my ducat awaited me.

In those days you had to climb the stairs, enter the second deck, then make your way back down to the box seats near first base. The sun had reached its zenith and was proceeding toward the high wall behind home plate, which would serve to shade those of us with means after the third inning or so. No such salvation awaited the bleacher bums, a solid mass of beer-swilling, peanut-cracking groundlings, many of whom would pass out from the combined effects of alcohol and heat stroke before the game was over. Meanwhile, the din they created in their agitation and discomfort nearly drowned out the more subdued discussions of the finer points of the game being conducted in the choice seats.

I spotted Teddy's gray locks and slid into the empty seat between him and Cuhulain. Teddy introduced us, and Cuhulain in turn introduced me to the man next to him.

"Jack Doyle, friend'o mine from Chicago" he said. "Jack's scoutin' for the Cubbys, he is."

Teddy and I leaned in to hear Doyle fill us in on the Cubs' pitching woes. Their bullpen was anchored by the aging Charlie Root, whose four run-plus ERA was indicative of the problems they were having.

"But Fette's a starter if he's anything," I said.

Doyle agreed, but pointed out that their starters left little to be desired. The number five guy, Curt Davis, had won six games. "I'm thinking Fette could be a long reliever," said Doyle. "Later in the season, when our starters get tired."

Having established our respective bona fides, we settled

in to watch the game. The first two Millers went down swinging, but number three, first baseman Joe Hauser, knocked Fette's first pitch out of the park. The roar that rose from the cheap seats was amazing. Half the rubes out there were from Minneapolis.

The dapper Cuhulain clapped hands in a restrained and gentlemanly way. "Credit where credit's due," he said, with a wink. "I admire the athlete, whilst largely ignorin' th' team."

I looked him over surreptitiously while Fette gouged the mound with his heel, and slapped the ball into his mitt in disgust. Cuhulain's hat remained on his head, cocked at a jaunty angle, despite the heat. He had smooth-shaven, olive skin, black eyebrows that grew together over the sort of Roman nose that certain sons of the old sod sport, and bright, intelligent eyes. His cravat was loosened, his starched collar was open at the throat. He put his elbow on his knee, rested his prominent chin on his fist, and watched Fette rear back and burn one down the middle for a strike.

What did that chin of his remind me of?—Ah yes, the Italian fellow, Il Duce. There must've been a legionnaire in Cuhulain's lineage. And a Celtic lass who knew which side her bread was buttered on.

The rhythm of the game soon established itself. By the time the sun passed behind the wall the crowd had quieted to concentrate on a pitching duel. Cuhulain and I shared some small talk while the batters whiffed or grounded out one after the other.

"See where Schmeling KOed Louis?" I said.

"Indeed, an' didn't I predict somethin'o the sort when I read that he was studyin' newsreels've the Bomber's minny triumphs last year," he replied.

He proceeded to explain his theory, which made perfect sense, as all theories about sporting events, politics, history, crime and anything else will, when presented after the fact. First of all, he pointed out, no boxer, least of all a heavyweight, has any business fighting thirteen times in a year. And since every move Louis made in all those fights was immortalized on celluloid, a boxer with the patience to analyze the film, and the skills to take advantage of what he learned, had a chance to beat him.

"The Bomber inntered the ring tired and flat, and Schmeling knew he dropped his left when he was fixin t'throw his right. I tuned in the fight, and every time Schmeling hit'im there came a great sound—WHACK! Ye'could hear it over the static. Tirrible noise, like a man smackin a side'a beef with a two-by-four. The Bomber was walkin' into those blows. He was a step late th'entire bout."

Suddenly the crowd rose to its feet and roared. Mickey Slade had walked while we were engrossed in conversation, and Fette himself had tied the game with a single that scored him.

"How d'ye like that, Jack," said Cuhulain to the scout. "A pitcher who can hit!"

"All due respect, we're lookin' for a pitcher who can pitch," said Doyle. "I heard yez discussin' the fight. Did you notice Tommy O'Rourke dropped dead in Schmeling's dressing room before it began?"

"Well, th'man was of an age t'kick the bookit," said Cuhulain.

I listened while they lionized one of the most controversial men in the fight business. O'Rourke, who was well into his eighties, had managed Joe Walcott, aka The Barbados Demon, back when whites and smokes were barred by gentleman's agreement from meeting in the ring. But O'Rourke was no gentleman. He saw to it that his fighter fought white boys, which earned him a certain amount of disapproval, although fans like myself generally thought of it as a good thing. O'Rourke had held many positions in the fight game over the years—boxer, trainer, manager, commissioner. He'd even been a judge at ringside when Jimmy McLarnin decisioned Barney Ross for the Welterweight title a few years back. He scored it for McLarnin, a dubious call that won back the hearts of his fellow Micks, many of whom had shunned him for managing Walcott.

I mentioned that I'd read of Capone's misadventure. Doyle hadn't seen that item, but Cuhulain had.

"I'll tell'ye this," he said. "If ye've the temerity t'stick a shiv in Snorty, ye'd be wise t'stick it in his heart. He's a bull of a man, and there's little forgiveness in him."

"That his moniker?" I inquired.—Among the initiated, 'Snorty' meant a darb and debonair demeanor back in those days.

He nodded in the affirmative. "Tis Alphonse's conceit that he's snorty," he explained. "It'd take a brave intrepid fillow t'tell him he's merely well-dressed."

"I've heard he doesn't like the Irish." I said.

"Nonsense," Cuhulain replied. "He cares not a wit whether a man were Irish, Eyetalian or Jew. What can'ye do for Snorty? is his question, and if the answer is nothin', then ye'd best give him a wide berth, regardless'a your origins.

"Tis a wonderful little burg ye'have here," he continued, and he tugged on Teddy's sleeve to make sure he overheard, "full of all the things that make life pleasurable an' fair burstin' with opportunity, but when it comes to talk'a th' Mick, th' Mocky, th' Hun, th' Dinge an'such, I find it a wee bit provincial. As for me, I'm aware that I'm reputed t'be a Mick mobster on the run from a crazy Wop, but nothin' could be further from the truth. Gimpy O'Banion was a friend'a mine, may he rest in peace, but we lived different lives. After his sad passin' I found Snorty t'be a sinsible, down to earth fillow, and not inclined t'let our rispictive allegiances get in th' way of an understandin.' St. Paul seemed th' best place fr'me, given th' particulars. Isn't that right, Teddy?"

"I've said it before, I'll say it again," Teddy replied. "You are the world's foremost authority on the affairs of Faennis Cuhulain."

"That I am, and we'll drink to it," said Cuhulain. He waved for the beer hawker.

Whilst we enjoyed our beers Cuhulain confided that Capone's successor, Paulie Ricca, had offered him the opportunity to "organize" St. Paul a few years back, meaning he'd be provided with some muscle to take over crime here.

"I declined, and advoised him aginst it," he said.

"'There's a gang in charge here already,' I says, 'and ye'd have to go t'war with'em. 'They can't be much,' says he, 'I nivir heard of'em.' 'Oh yes ye have,' says I. 'They call themselves 'The Police.'"

I asked him whether Ricca let it go at that, or offered the turf to someone else.

"I thought it best not t'inquire," he replied.

Doyle left during the seventh inning stretch, with Fette still throwing, and protecting a safe lead. He'd walked one, struck out five and allowed two hits, both home runs. Doyle was noncommital, but I was pretty sure we'd seen the last of Steady Lou.

After the Saints batted in the eighth, and scored another run, Teddy suggested we leave as well, to avoid traffic. He was anxious to show off his brand new touring sedan.

Amazingly in this crowd of thousands, he ran into several fellows he knew on the way out, and paused to glad hand them. McGlaughin winked at me, as if to say, "that's our Teddy."

He'd parked a few blocks away on Fuller Street, which was lined with cars, but Teddy's was easily spotted. It was a royal blue Fleetwood, thirty feet long if it was an inch, featuring a vented hood topped by a winged silver ornament, and four doors that opened at the middle of the chassis, like French Windows.

Teddy opened the curbside rear door, and revealed opera-style back seats. There was enough leg room for Primo Carnera. He bade the two of us be seated.

"I'll just take us on a tour of our provincial little burg," he said. "You ride in the rear like gentlemen."

He drove down Lexington Avenue, and turned east on Summit. As we cruised past the brownstones, Cuhulain expanded on the concept of "snorty" as applied to Chicago gangsters. He confessed to a veneer of snortiness himself, and even conceded that his natty duds and ornate locutions were a relic of the snorty habits he'd acquired when he palled around with Dion "Gimpy" O'Banion, the snortiest of them all.

"Gimpy certainly provoked Alphonse's wrath concernin' business on minny occasions," he said, "but I'll always believe Capone had him murthered because he possessed a natural sophistication that got under our Eyetalian friend's skin."

O'Banion, he explained, had a ready smile, a beautiful tenor voice and a deceptively gentle manner. He was always impeccably dressed and carefully groomed, right down to the neatly manicured six inch long nail on the little finger of his left hand, the mark of a Chicago rosco who'd never stooped to hand labor more arduous than pulling a trigger.

"He was always smilin, Gimpy was, always glad t'see ye. He'd look a man in th'eye, tell him he was a fine fillow, and a minute later tell Hymie t' rub him out."

According to Cuhulain, this coldly elegant manner of O'Banion's became the sine qua non of snorty in twenties Chicago.

O'Banion's hit man, Hymie Weiss, had an odd snortiness of his own, grounded in an inexplicable quirk. A Catholic of Polack extraction, he took a Hebe nom de guerre just for the snorty hell of it. If you asked why, he might smile and say nothing, or he might pull out a pistol and shoot you.

"Hymie was the only man in Chicago Capone feared," said Cuhulain, "and that were his death warrant. Snorty is not the type t'live in fear, y'see, so he had Hymie killed. He's like Gimpy was in that respect. They'd both kill on a whim. As fr'me, God willin' I'll get through life without blood on me hands."

I told him that was my wish as well. Cuhulain was a spellbinder and could obviously go on forever about Chicago. I waited patiently for an opening while we descended Ramsey Hill and turned on to Smith Street. As we crossed the High Bridge Cuhulain was in the midst of explaining what a great lover of flowers O'Banion was, and how he took pleasure in operating the florist shop that served as headquarters for his rackets. He said that O'Banion personally designed the wreaths he provided for the grand funerals that were thrown for fallen Chicago gangsters.

From there he slid seamlessly into a recollection of his maiden Aunt's annual pilgrimage to Newgrange, twelve kilometers from their humble sod home in County Meath, to place a garland of wildflowers on the ancient cairn. That was the way the old folks celebrated the vernal equinox in that neck of the woods, he explained.

"She took a carriage there, didn't she, bless her old heart." A tear slid down his cheek. "She called the day 'The Alban Eilir,' in the auld tongue."

He finally paused in his narrative to admire the forested bluffs of the Mississippi.

"You're in the flower business yourself, I'm told," I said.

He squinted at me as if he were studying some rare plant.

"'Told,' are'ye? Now who'd be tellin'ye that?"

"To be honest," I lied, "I can't remember. I've been talkin' to so many people lately. I'm a private detective."

"That's what our mutual friend Mr. Eccles E S Q up there tells me. He didn't tell me ye were talkin' t'people about my affairs, though. But then he's a devious sort, aren't ye Teddy?"

He leaned forward, nudged Teddy, and repeated his query.

"I am" Teddy agreed, over his shoulder. "How else could I be such a roaring success in these hard times?"

"I'm interested in your business only as it relates to a case I'm working on, Faennis," I told him. "I've been hired to find out who murdered Bobby Tuttweiler."

"Ah." He was silent for awhile.

"A sad day that was, when Bobby fell. We won't be seein' the likes'o him again. I've no compunction about talkin' t'ye about that matter, McDonough. I'd like t'see the bastard who murthered Bobby hung by th' heels and flayed alive. As far as my affairs are concerned, ye've a reputation fr'discretion and ye'wouldn't want to go spoilin' it, now would ye?"

I assured him I wouldn't.

He explained that his relationship with Bobby came about as an offshoot of his deal with Capone. It had begun when the Feds started using the Internal Revenue Act against mobsters, and money laundering became a lucrative occupation. Gangsters on the east coast used the tomato business to legitimize their loot, but any form of produce purchased for cash in large, untraceable quantities would do.

"I'd been buyin' flowers fr'Gimpy fr'years by the time he were murthered," he said, "an' if ye've ever seen a flower market ye'll know why it couldn't be better for the purpose. If ye try t'give a flower monger a check they'll laugh in your face. I told Snorty I could make cash presentable to the revenuers by buyin' flowers. An' of course I took mine off the top."

He explained the process of money laundering. Most of it went in one ear and out the other, but I got the basics. Purchase something with funds illegitimately acquired, sell it for publicly circulated money and document the sale according to your specifications. Mobsters expected to lose something in the wash, which was why a man in Cuhulain's shoes stood to make plenty, but each method of laundering had its own peculiar problems. Produce rots, for example, so if you launder cash in New York by buying thousands of pounds of tomatoes, many will go soft before they're sold. The only recourse is to make sauce, which, according to Cuhulain, explains why hundreds of spaghetti joints had sprung up all over the five boroughs.

"I grew to envy those fillows," he said. "Meself, I was eternally dealin' with the same auld problem. A bloom is good for three days, maybe five in a cooler. Then there's nothin' t'be done. It was gettin' so I couldn't sell flowers fast enough to clean up Snorty's money, an' others were comin' t'me as well. Dillinger's roscoes had begun usin' my services. I was at the end'a me rope when a florist I was dealin' with put a boog in me ear. 'Get on the train and take yerself a trip up to St. Paul,' he said. 'It's a wee little city, but they sell more flowers there than we do here, an'there's but one man behind it'."

That man was Bobby Tuttweiler, and as Cuhulain explained how he and Bobby prospered together I began to better understand the odd dynamics of the Tuttweiler family.

Cuhulain had seen the numbers before he came here. What the florist told him was literally true. There were more flowers sold in St. Paul than Chicago, and most of them were roses.

"Bobby were the progenitor'a the industry," he said. "This happened before my time here, but it's my understandin' that the local flower business sprung directly from his loins, so to speak. When he started sellin' flowers there were just a few shops, all of'em run by men, and other men come around t'buy when they had to, fr'anniverarys an'weddings an' such. Bobby put women behind the counter, because he figured men would come around and buy from the ladies more often, an' right he were."

Cuhulain admitted that he'd arrived with a notion of simply taking over Chicago-style, but quickly realized he was dealing with a one-man show. Nor was it necessary to muscle in. Bobby was in it for romance. Money was practically an afterthought. His life revolved around setting women up at florist shops, running their business for them because when they were happy he was happy, and making love to them. He serviced a few shops a day, a dozen or so a week, and used his suite at the St. Paul Hotel as a place to enjoy long rendevous, as opposed to the back room quickies that were his stock in daily trade.

Bobby's customers were forever telling him he should go into business for himself, but he was content working for Midland, where he could expense his predilections and not bother with the intricacies of wholesaling—with one exception. He used his charm to talk wealthy men into investing, because he knew how to create demand, but cash for supply was a recurring problem. Until Cuhulain came along.

"Bobby could sell as minny blooms as ye'could provide him with," said Cuhulain. "I can tell'ye I were happy as a pig in shite when I seen how our interests dovetailed."

Cuhulain got to know Bobby well, and they began to pal around because of their shared taste in what he termed, "th' foiner things." He was soon introduced to Betty Tuttweiler, and noticed that she was one of those things.

"Bobby were a sophisticated fillow, an my relationship with his wife was somethin' we acknowledged, but rarely spoke of," he said.

He smiled as he recollected one occasion when they'd spoken of it.

"Betty'd often spent a night'r two in me rooms up at the St. Paul Hotel, an' one mornin' she bumped into Bobby and a lady friend of his in the hall. Bobby couldn't help laughin when he told me of it. They all rode the lift together, y'see, and it got a bit stiff. Bobby had quite a sense'a humor, he did. Told marvelous jokes, and not even a wee bit smutty they were."

He shook his sadly.

"Betty's a lovely woman," he added. "I still see her occasionally." He smiled, and continued his story.

Because Cuhulain's arrival in St. Paul created a new supply of money, Bobby, who was never at a loss, set about creating a new demand. Until then, florists simply dumped their stale blooms and factored the price of waste into the flowers they sold. It was Bobby's genius to see the potential that represented.

"Poets have observed that the beauty of a rose is niver more exquisite than the moment it begins to wilt," Cuhulain explained, in his, dare I say it, flowery fashion. "A fillow might buy that rose on impulse, whereras, given time to peruse at leisure, he'd be inclined t'select somethin' a bit less mature. Now Bobby knew flowers an' th' business of flowers as well as anyone, but he were a true expert—and a poet t'boot—when it came t'women. He was aware that unlike a rose, the beauty of a woman is niver more poignant than the moment it bursts from the bud, so t'speak, an' if a man were ever to purchase a bloom impulsively, twould be in the presence of such beauty."

Or, stated simply, it was Bobby's idea to put nubile girls on the street selling moribund roses in order to turn excess inventory into cash. Overnight a new market was created, along with a method for laundering thousands more per week. As Cuhulain proceeded to explain, Bobby stumbled on it in his own way.

"He weren't the kind'a man t'be gettin in the knickers of a sixteen year old lass, but he did succumb t'that temptation once. Twere a friend of his dotter's. Then in a proper fit'a remorse he went t'the priest."

"He confessed?"

"Of course not. The man wasn't daft. He had a scheme. Two of 'em. Absolution and business. He devised his own act'a contrition, an' got the priest in on it without tellin' him why, so's to make it legal and bindin' on the Lard."

He explained that Bobby devised a plan in which poor parish families, most of whom had many children, including at least one teen-aged daughter, could make some money. He started collecting roses on the verge of wilting from his retail customers, and giving them to the girls. They sold them on the street for a nickel each, and split the proceeds with Bobby.

"He'd give a little'a that back t'the florists. That made the florists happy, an' not shy'a orderin' more than they might sell. He niver took a penny from the lass he wronged though. Gave her as minny roses as she could sell. Told me layin' with her was the worst sin he'd ever committed in a lifetime'a philanderin'. His dotter never forgave him, even though the lass said she were none the worse for it."

"Sounds like that girl's family might've had reason to take a shotgun to him," I observed.

"I've pondered minny possibilities since he was murthered, includin' that one. T'th'best'a me knowledge, her's was a humble family, an' thought it a foin thing t'have their dotter sullied by Mr. Tuttweiler. No, there're more likely suspects."

"Coppers think it was the guy who owned Midland. You heard about the key man insurance?"

"Heard of it? I collected it," he said, without a moment's hesitation.

He explained that Slansky had pestered him to fork over set sums on a regular basis, ideally a quarterly investment, so he could plan purchases ahead. Cuhulain knew that this was not unreasonable, but he also knew that if Slansky lost Bobby, Midland Wholesale Florists was useless as a money laundry.

"Mr. Slansky and I came to an agreement," he said. "I gave him his quarterly invistmint, but he purchased a key man insurance policy, an' agreed that if anything happened t'Bobby the money were mine. Bobby didn't know that I were behind buyin' that policy, or that I had a financial interest in it. When he strook out on his own— which Betty'd been after him t'do, but I never thought he would—Slansky wanted t'drop the insurance. 'No,' I told him, 'Bobby'll come back, mark my words,' an' in my opinion he would've. Of course Betty and Bobby were angry at Slansky over him keepin' the policy. Too bad, but twere nothin' to be done."

"And of course you know that makes you a prime suspect," I said.

"I do indeed, but the theory rests on a false assumption. I were doin' business with Bobby after he left Midland, an' he were worth minny thousands more t'me alive than dead. Not t'mention the fact that I'd cut off me arm before I'd raise it against him.... After Bobby were made they broke the mold. What a lovely an'worldly fillow. An' t'think I run into him in a rustic little backwater like this one."

He took a handkerchief out of his breast pocket and dabbed at his eye. If you want to know what kind of man he was, the fact that it didn't strike me as a false gesture is as good a description as I can offer.

"Think Slansky killed him?"

"If he did it were fr'spite not money. Excuse me." He blew his nose, and returned the hanky to his pocket. "A'course, if I had a dime for every man in Chicago that were killed fr'spite I'd retire.—Nah, I don't think so. He isn't a killer."

Cuhulain said he'd paid Slansky's legal expenses on condition that Slansky push his lawyer to collect on the policy. I asked if he'd used the insurance to buy flowers.

"Nota-tall," he said. "I've slowed down the money washin' commensurate with the situation—Prohibition gone, Snorty in stir. Paulie Ricca and I used to do quite a lot've business, but there's not so minny blooms sold nowadays, are there? The stale ones still go out on the streets, but the hawkers have t'make their own deals with the florists, an'there's hundreds of hawkers now, lasses, lads, ten year old boys, old gents, all of'em competin' with each other, so that's not so lucrative as it once was. Nor is th' market so lively. People have caught on, y'see. They want fresh blooms, not somethin' that fades two hours after they bought it. But if th' hawkers are sellin' fresh roses, then th' florists are competin' with themselves, aren't they?"

I asked him how he dealt with that.

"By retirin'," he replied. "I'm pretty well fixed innyway. Only one thing I needed t'take care of, an' that's done. The insurance money were paid out last March. Came in the nick'a time. I called Betty the day I got it, and told her I were comin' over t'give'er a gift of flowers on The Alban Eilir, accordin' to the old traditions.—Y'know, Bobby were the type'a fillow t'spend ivery penny without a thought for th'morrow, an' there weren't much left after he were gone. Betty was lookin' pretty tense by then, him in the ground ten months an' her not knowin' where t'turn.—I'll niver forget the look on her face when I handed her a bouquet all wrapped in florist's paper, and inside among the flowers were an envelope containin' the insurance money. Ivery penny of it."

After she'd collapsed in his arms and thanked him, he'd seized the moment to confess that he was behind the purchase of the key man policy. He explained why, and told her the money was rightfully hers.

My mind was reeling from revelation overload by then. I caught Teddy's eye in the mirror and signaled it was time to bring things to a conclusion, but Cuhulain wasn't ready to call it a day. He continued to praise the Tuttweilers, both the quick and the dead, as we headed for the hotel. When we got there he invited us up for a drink.

His suite was on the third floor overlooking St. Peter Street, which was empty except for a few poor souls on the bum who'd forgotten how seriously we take the Sabbath around here. Nary a bottle to be purchased, nor a working stiff to panhandle.

Cuhulain took a fifth of Jameson's out of a drawer, poured us each a glass neat, and busied himself tuning in a concert on the Philco, all the while bemoaning the sorry state of music in the U.S.A.

"What've we here?" he said. "Why it's the Blue Network, and the illustrious Victor Herbert inflictin' his sorry self upon our ears."

He fiddled with the dial nonetheless, and eliminated the static just in time for a Lux Soap ad.

"I hesitate t'ponder what pleasures await us on the Red Network," he mumbled, "Perhaps the mel-lowjious Lawrence Tibbets. Or God help us, Nelson Eddy ...." He turned the volume down to background level.

"Of course," said Teddy, "only the great McKormack -"

"Now none'a your wisecracks, Mr Eccles E S Q. I've yet to take'ye t'task for puttin'me together with a private eye who's probin' a matter that concerns me. I'm trustin' this man with me life."—He nodded in my direction—"I'm not just beatin' me gums either. I'm well acquainted with the minny ways death can sneak up, an' it often begins like this.—No offense, mind'ye."

"None taken," I said.

"What do you mean?" asked Teddy.

He pondered the question briefly, while Victor Herbert, whom a Mocky client of mine once described as "the divine schmalz herring," followed his secret heart.

"What I mean," said Cuhulain, "is that a man might say somethin' fr'simple love'a tellin' a story, an' it comes around an' whacks him a tirrible blow from behind. A man such as Martin here might give his sources away inadvertently, fr'example. Let on he knows somethin' when there's only one way he could know it, an' that might put his source in danger."

I told him I understood. He rubbed his chin and looked me over.

"I believe ye do. So that takes care'a that. But, as each of ye' know from your own occupations, there're other ways t'set the fatal thing in motion. Ye might talk casually of people ye don't think of as dangerous, ye may even go ahead an'rub shoulders with'em, but if ye'd given it a moment's thought ye'd realize ye'd underestimated the danger they represent."

Teddy nodded. "I only take clients on reference from people I trust now. Too many 'bingers.'"

"Meanin'?" Cuhulain asked.

"Meaning men who spent time in solitary confinement, and came out 'binged,' in jailbird lingo. It doesn't take much for an inmate to be put in solitary nowadays. The penitentiaries have no budget, no staff, so they use the threat of it to keep order. Crack wise to a guard, try to sneak some food out of the mess hall, get in a fist fight, off you go for a long time. Fellows lose their minds in solitary, and most of'em eventually get out of the pen. Back a few years ago, when all you had to do to engage my services was walk in the door and give your name to my secretary, a few bingers ended up in my office telling me they'd done some foolish thing and were desperate not to go back to stir. You can't talk rationally to people like that, but you can't promise you'll save them either. One fellow took a swing at me. Another said he'd hunt me down and shoot me if I didn't take his case and win it."

Cuhulain nodded. "Well, there ye'have it. We all know t'watch who we're dealin' with.—So then, what do ye make of Bobby's murther?" he asked me.

"This is the first I've heard that Bobby was connected to gangsters. I gotta think about that for awhile."

"It'd be overstatin' the case considerably t'say he were cinnicted t'gangsters. He were cinnicted t'me, an'I were cinnicted t'gangsters."

I smiled amiably. "All due respect, you love to tell a tale. I imagine Bobby and the roscoes you wash money for got to know quite a bit about each other over the years you and Bobby did business."

"But I were always conscious'a the risks. And so was he. Bobby niver rubbed shoulders with the roscoes. It disgusted him th' way people around here talk about 'em, and point'em out on the street like they're somethin' grand. So ye'd be barkin' up the wrong tree."

I shrugged. "I'm always hearing someone is connected to gangsters. I check it out, they rarely are. This is different though. No one said Bobby had even the remotest connection to gangsters. Now it turns out he did."

He continued to insist that connecting the murder to gangsters was a dead end. I agreed it probably was, but who else did Bobby rub shoulders with that might commit such a crime?

We ran through jealous husbands and jilted lovers. He dismissed them the same way Marcie had. Everybody loved Bobby. They couldn't help it. We chewed over the fact that he was murdered when he opened the door for someone who must have come under the guise of doing business, hence the roses on the floor. That brought it back to Slansky, but neither of us believed he did it.

Then Cuhulain had a thought. He said that the priest that helped Bobby devise the rose hawker scheme suggested that the poorer parish boys be given a chance to sell flowers as well. Bobby was reticent, but the priest insisted.

"Some'a them lads were trouble," Cuhulain said. "I recognized the type from me Chicago days. Street scrappers, rounders, cannon fodder fr' the mob, that's how I viewed'em. Snorty n'Gimpy used t'keep ten or twelve of'em on the payroll just t'make life miserable fr'each other. After Bobby opened his shop, a few of those lads couldn't get it through their thick heads that the flowers had t'come from retail florists, an' then only when they were stale. Couldn't get the scheme straight! Or maybe they could, an' they didn't like it. They were fr'ever pestering Bobby fr' fresh blooms at a price. Could one'a them've come knockin' that mornin'? Who knows. I nivir give a thought t'that end'a the business, it were in such capable hands. Maybe if I'd paid more attintion he'd be with us today "

He dabbed at his eye with his handkerchief again.—"Ah, what's the sense in keenin' when the funeral's over," he said, raising his glass. "T'Bobby Tuttweiler."

We drank to the deceased, then sat for awhile, lost in our own thoughts. Gradually, a low howl from the Philco intruded on our musings. It sounded like a malfunction related to the vacuum tubes. Cuhulain patted the side of the machine firmly. When that didn't halt it he tinkered with the tuner, until he realized it was only Jeanette McDonald, emoting the dread Indian Love Call—"When I'm calling youuu- hooo-hoo-hoo -"

He snapped it off in disgust. "So then, Martin, where'll your inquiries take'ye next?" he asked

"Maybe to the priest." I held out my glass for a refill.

"Ye're in luck," he said, as he poured. "He'll be presidin' at the weddin'."

"What wedding?"

"Ye hadn't heard? It come up kind of sudden. Bobby Jr. is marryin.' An well, I'm told."

"I forgot to tell you, Martin," said Teddy. "I only found out yesterday myself. He's marrying into the White Bear Ervines. Very wealthy family."

"Bobby often told me he wanted his children t'marry rich," said Cuhulain

"He's marryin' rich and beautiful if she's the gal I'm thinkin' of," I said.

"I've heard she frequents Kuby's," said Teddy. "Just between us, her family doesn't like that at all. Kuby's is a dive. The D A tells me they sniff nose candy there."

"They do indeed," I said. "Can either'a you gents wangle me an invite to the wedding? Otherwise I'll have to find another way to approach the priest."

"Ah, don't worry yourself," said Cuhulain. According to him the wedding was a private affair, but it was come one come all for the reception, which would be held in a banquet room at this very hotel. "Th' priest'll certainly be there, sociable fillow that he is."

Everything seemed to be falling into place. I'd talk to the priest. He'd give me the low down on Wigger, Tipper and sundry other scrappers, rounders and nose candy sniffers, all of whom Eddy Guifoyle had managed to ignore when he investigated the murder. Marcie would be there. I could set up another meeting. My only regret was that it might be our last.

The three of us spent the rest of the afternoon talking baseball, boxing, and finally the war that everyone feared was brewing.

"It doesn't concern this country," said Teddy."We should stay out."

"Maybe, but we'll get dragged in anyway," was my reply.

"What do you think, Faennis?" Teddy asked.

He didn't answer directly. Instead, he sang us a verse to the tune of 'O Christmas Tree', a ditty that he said was all the rage in the old country when he'd emigrated, twenty years past, on the eve of The War To End All Wars:

"Ah Germany, sweet Germany, why don't ye come set Ireland free?"

A Moral Failing

Next evening found me at Tin Cup's, in the unique position of being on speaking terms with both Eddy Guilfoyle and Slapper Doran. Eddy was at the far end of the bar by himself, staring into his drink. I made a point of greeting him. He muttered hello, but was in no mood to converse. He'd lost more weight, and looked like he needed ironing.

Doran was in his usual booth near the front door, whispering with a couple of his boys. They peered at me like I was interrupting an IRA meeting.

"Whadda you want, McDonough?" snarled the pride of Slap's stable, Myron "My" Sullivan, a welterweight said to be in line for a title shot at Madison Square Garden.

Normally you don't need an appointment to talk with Slapper, who came by his moniker by slapping you on the back to get your attention if he thought you weren't fixated on him. I ignored Sullivan and addressed him directly.

"Gimme a few minutes of your precious time," I said. "Maybe we can help each other."

He told his boys to take a walk. They complied in reasonably good spirits, and posted themselves at the bar where they could cast menacing looks at Eddy. He sneered back once, then ignored them. I ordered us a couple drinks.

"Heard'ya had some bad luck," I said.

"Luck had nothin' to do with it. Your friend over there trapped me. That's what my lawyer says."

"Really? I heard it was you that trapped somebody, after Eddy put the squeeze on'ya. One'a those Huns I saw you with at Kuby's."

He registered some surprise that I'd seen him at Kuby's, but not much. He was preoccupied with the injustice of his predicament.

"Same thing," he said. "Eddy sends Little Mikey after me, pretty soon I'm back to the wall. What choice do I have?"

"You can clam up. They can put you in the dock, but they can't make you talk."

"Yeh yeh yeh. Then I take the fall."

"Bingo."

"Jee-zus McDonough! I thought'ya said ya could help me! I can help myself do five years in the can.—Jee- ZUS!"

"Just drawin' the picture. Here's what I have in mind. You tell me a few things about that fellow you trapped, I talk to somebody who knows the D A."

Doran was no fool. He asked the obvious question.

"Uh uh, no guarantees," I replied, "just a bug in somebody's ear."

He blustered and whined, but soon adopted the right attitude—what do I have to lose?

He told me he'd met Danny Wegleitner, aka Wigger, on Rice Street one evening about a year ago, selling flowers. They got to talking. Wigger told him that along with the roses he had some candy that he might sell to a few special customers. Slapper decided to try some. Wasn't long before he'd acquired a sweet tooth, but not much of one according to him.

He asked me if I was investigating the so-called dope ring that Eddy G had smashed, which, he assured me, was a figment of Eddy's cop imagination.

"I'm not interested in dope rings," I told him. "This Wigger character is maybe involved in somethin' else I'm nosin' around about."

He was curious, but I let him know who was asking the questions, and put a few more to him. He said he didn't know much about Wigger, but remembered him saying that he'd been in stir for awhile, and would've stayed longer if not for the help of a pen pal.

"He told me they weren't gonna turn him loose unless he had work, which was pretty hopeless what with the Depression and all," Slapper explained, "but this dame, this pen pal'a his, got him a job."

"What dame?"

He didn't know her name, but he knew her father was in the flower business. Then his face lit up. "So that's what you're investigatin'! I heard the guy was murdered. You don't think Wigger—"

"Don't get ahead'a yourself," I advised him.

The mere thought of being connected, even peripherally,

to something as exciting as murder made Slapper forget his troubles. Instead of me pulling information out of him grudgingly, he started racking his brain for more. Some of it was helpful.

Wigger had been out of stir for six months or so when he and Slapper met, and yes, he had been romantically involved with his former pen pal, but their love didn't blossom immediately. They'd started sparking about the same time Slapper got to know him.

"I see her with him at Kuby's," he said. "Told me he was gone on her. I don't blame him, she's a knockout, but a little while ago he tells me that just as sudden as she got a crush on him, bang—it's all over."

"And this happened when?"

"Few weeks, maybe a month ago."

"Name's Angie, right?"

"Yeh yeh yeh, now ya mention it. Angie."

I told Slapper he'd been very helpful, but he wasn't ready to let go. He commiserated about his situation, and told me yet again that the nose candy ring was malarkey.

"So I whiffed a little snow, what of it?" he said. "That son of a bitch,"—he pointed at Eddy, not surreptitiously, but with wagging finger and outstretched arm—"is tellin' everybody there's this big buncha people in cahoots, and I'm sellin' the stuff. Lies! I give some snow to a guy referees matches at the Auditorium. Once. That's it. Eddy says there's a gang operatin' outta Kuby's, claims I'm sellin' it around the parish, even arrested some dinge who's supposed to bring it over from Rondo -"

"What dinge?"

"Guy plays piano, can't remember his name. Hey hey hey, he in on the flower guy drop? Tell me, McDonough, c'mon."

"His name Sean?"

"Yeh yeh yeh Sean. God's my witness I don't know nothin' about dope rings, I -

"Nice talkin' to you, Slap. I'll see what I can do."

Slap's boys rejoined him as soon as I left the booth. They leaned in and conspired. I took one of the stools they'd vacated and kept an eye on the imaginative Mr. G.

Eddy was never a guy to close the bar down. Best I could recall from taking casual note of his habits, he was home in the loving arms of Mrs. G by ten p. m. After awhile I stationed myself near the door, next to the Mighty Wurlitzer, and watched for signs of his imminent departure.

"Fill your pockets up with some—sunshine and flowers," crooned Crosby. "If you want the things you love— you must have showers --ba-baboo..."

John O'Connor came over to strike up a conversation. I invented a headache to explain why I wasn't my usual garrulous self.

"Try Carter's Pills," John suggested.

"But that's for your liver, isn't it?" I couldn't help replying.

"Tis your liver," John explained. "Liver'n lights, they're all connected to the seat of pain, and that's behind your eyes, Martin." He tapped his own noggin for emphasis. "My dad explained it. Just before he died."

Had I been as eager to engage as I normally am, I'd surely have pursued that line of inquiry. His father, John O'Connor Sr., former chief of the St. Paul Police, had trod the same well-worn path I was treading and if anyone knew about the associated maladies it was him. Unfortunately duty beckoned. I massaged my temples and mutely feigned the throes of a thumper. John drifted away. Soon I saw Eddy wave the barman off when he came to check.

I slipped out the door and waited.

A fliver rumbled past, then another a few minutes later. Enough time passed so I wondered if I'd jumped the gun. I walked across the street and stood in a doorway so's I wouldn't bump into anyone I knew.

The two bulbs in the Tin Cup's sign that burned out the day after Prohibition was repealed still hadn't been replaced. Several more had dimmed noticeably. Nevertheless, there was enough light to see who came and went.

Bertie Crimmins, a belligerent hoocher even by Rice Street standards, staggered out and looked around for someone to insult. The street was empty and I wasn't visible, so he wove his way down the block toward Mooney's.

Having nothing better to do, I mentally reconstructed the previous few minutes of Bertie's evening—draining his glass, swiping the back of his hand across his flattened beezer, loudly demanding one on the house, cursing the bar, the bar man and everyone in the bar upon being turned down, and slowly revolving on his bar stool in search of an antagonist. His eyes would have fallen on Doran's booth, but he isn't that screwy. The clientele at Mooney's was older and more to his liking.

A few minutes later Eddy strode out, paused to spark a gasper, and started down the street. I caught up to him at the corner.

"Got a minute, Eddy?"

He wore his weariness of me, of the Tuttweiler case and the many new and different forms of corruption to which it had introduced him, of life in general, like an ill-fitting overcoat. It looked awful but it was big enough to duck in.

"New twist in the Tuttweiler case, Eddy."

"Told'ja, I never want to hear about that again."

He started to leave, but I caught him by the arm.

"You should listen."

"Get your hands off me," he said. "Talk. Make it quick."

"I'll make it quick as I can, but there's some things we gotta cover. Number one, the smoke you collared? Turn him loose. I'm gonna check down at the lockup tomorrow, and he better be gone."

A little of the old flash showed in his eyes. "Who the hell are you to tell me -"

I told him I was the guy who knew he slept with Betty Tuttweiler, so he should keep his best interests in mind. He took a drag, dropped his butt on the sidewalk, and carefully ground it out with his size 12 brogan.

"Whatta you care about that dinge?" he inquired, without much conviction.

I said I had it on good authority that the dinge in question wouldn't touch snow with a barge pole, and anyway

I needed to talk to him. Eddy knew I had him by the short hairs, but he managed a feeble counter.

"They let'cha visit guys in the can. Talk to him there. He's key to makin' my case."

"Case? Y'mean that nose candy ring you dreamed up? Listen, I'm willing to assume, for argument's sake, that you might be pursuing justice for Bobby Tuttweiler your own way, and all things bein' equal I don't wanna wreck your life—but..."

I let it hang.

"'But' what?"

"But Marcie Kirkwood hired me to find out who killed her father and I'm just about there. Best thing you can do is make things easy. I'll take care of you if I can. Maybe you won't lose your job."

He claimed, not very convincingly, that he didn't need anyone taking care of him. What he'd done with Betty Tuttweiler was immoral, he admitted. And failing to confess it was worse.

"But it ain't unethical," he said. "No reason it should cost me my job."

He was on shaky ground and he knew it. Not that the ethical duty of a St. Paul copper wasn't a fluid concept, but crimes against ordinary citizens were supposed to be pursued impartially.

"No reason you should lose your job?" I countered. "Betty Tuttweiler stands to collect twenty large if the murder is pinned on Slansky, you sleep with her, do everything in your power to put him in the dock, and that's ethical?"

"He had motive and opportunity. He's the obvious suspect."

"But we both know he didn't do it."

He didn't say anything for awhile, then asked what I wanted. I wasn't sure yet, I said, but step one was turning Sean loose.

"I can't just walk in and unlock the door. I told the D A he was part of a dope ring."

"Figure somethin' out."

"It'll take time, maybe a week."

I agreed to that. He hung around and talked a few minutes, told me that Betty Tuttweiler had been on him from the day of the murder to arrest Sheldon Slansky, and never let up. She called four-five times a week, wheedled and pleaded, met him for drinks, told him she'd lose her home, that she'd have to sell flowers on the street. But the more he investigated, the less likely it seemed that Slansky was the killer.

"Ever come up with another suspect?" I asked.

"Nah. I looked into some people. The gal who discovered his body, some associates'a his. Led nowhere."

I told him I was surprised an investigator of his caliber hadn't discovered anything in all this time, as much as called him a liar, but he didn't take the bait. Then, as we were about to part, he blurted out the confession he'd been aching to make for more than a year. It didn't take long, but it contained a detail that revealed why he'd have had a tough time telling a priest.

"It was Ash Wednesday," he said, "right after morning

Mass. Betty left a message at the precinct, said come over soon as I could, she had some new information. But there was nothin' new, just more talk've the key man policy, her fear of livin' on handouts. She poured us a drink, cried. I tried to comfort her..."

He paused with a look on his face as if he would burst into tears himself. "The mark of the ash was still on my forehead when I laid with her, Martin. God'll never forgive me."

A Joyous Occasion

Maybe not, but Father Krause would. I met the earthy prelate of St. Albert's a few days later, at the gala reception that followed the Tuttweiler/Ervine nuptials. He had a big grin, a goatee, and a fringe of razor-cut hair around the balding crown of his head. His charcoal grey vestment was trimmed with silver piping, and tailored to hang just so.

"Call me Russ," he said when I introduced myself. He laid an arm on my shoulder and nudged me along as he used his collar to buffalo our way to the front of the drink line.

"Come on over here where we can talk," he said, after we picked up a couple whiskey and waters. He led us to a dimly lit corner where the sound of the band (which still lacked its regular piano player) was softened, and we were unlikely to be interrupted.

"Bobby would have loved this," he told me. "Classy crowd, classy venue, good hooch, everything he wanted for his son. He prayed every day that his children would marry well. Such a shame he didn't live to see this. You know, he'd had his eye on this family and this very young lady for a long time."

I had my eye on her too, since I realized she was not the curvy blonde who'd been hanging all over Bobby. Kate Tuttweiler, nee Ervine, was the gal with the snow habit that Sean had pointed out at Kuby's. She was a tall, flat-chested, auburn-haired frail who appeared to be dazed by the pro-ceedings, which, I'd been told by a fellow celebrant, had been planned and executed in such haste that he assumed she was pregnant.

If she was, it was too early to show. Viewed from the re-ception line, the bride was exquisitely groomed, expensive-ly coiffed, flat-bellied and semi-beautiful. At handshake distance she appeared tense and run-over. The wooden smile pasted on her otherwise severe mug ticked a fleet-ing acknowledgment when I wished her the best. She kept swiping at her nose.

I told Bobby he could still be a crooner when we shook hands. That seemed to please him.

"Isn't she lovely," said Russ.

"No. But I'm sure she's suitable in all the important ways."

He acknowledged the truth of that with a fleeting smile. "So. Tell me more about yourself," he said. "I find detective work fascinating."

"What's there to say, Russ? I went to St. Thomas for a year, thought about joining the police and decided to be-come a private eye instead. It's worked out pretty well."

"Ever kill a man?"

"Uh-uh."

"Just curious."

"I get that question all the time."

"And the family hired you to find out who killed Bobby?"

"Marcella hired me. The others just want to put it behind them. They think they know who killed him, but they're afraid he'll never be convicted."

Russ ate up this kind of gossip, I could see that. He told me that Betty had never confided in him, but he'd heard through the grapevine that a Hebe murdered Bobby, for money. I said my inquiries led me to believe otherwise. He whistled softly and asked who done it.

"I'm not sure yet," I replied, "but I've got a theory. I'd like to tell you about it. Maybe you could help."

"Of course, of course, go ahead."

I said it would best if we discussed it in more private circumstances. "I'll call soon," I told him.

"Maybe a little hint about where your investigation is leading?"

I declined with a smile and excused myself.

I'd taken barely a step when I bumped into Amy, the gal I'd seen with Bobby not so long ago at the family home. She was luscious as ever.

"Amy?" I said.

She looked at me blankly until I reminded her where we'd met, and whom she'd been with. "This isn't a very happy occasion for you, is it, dear?" I asked.

She seemed confused by the question. "Why?" she finally replied.

"Well, you and Bobby seemed pretty tight, I thought -"

"Oh, I get it." She favored me with a wicked little grin. "I don't think I've seen the last of Bobby."

I noticed Russ staring at us with what might have been a lascivious look in his eye. I introduced the two of them and excused myself.

I caught a glimpse of Marcie and The Lucky Dog among a group I took to be the Ervine clan. Like the others in that crowd, Marcie looked more bemused than joyful on this joyous occasion. I was making my way in her direction when Angie took my arm, planted a kiss on my cheek and squired me toward the buffet table. I told her whiskey killed my appetite, but she was having none of it.

"C'mon, grab a plate, sit with me," she insisted.

She speared a few slices of roast beef for me, spooned on some salad and potatoes, filled her own plate, and found us a table on the Tuttweiler's side of the room.

The band was playing a rendition of Hold That Tiger, featuring a vigorous solo by a drunk trumpet player. Between the music and the din of voices it was hard to make small talk. Betty waved from a nearby table. Angie leaned in close so I could hear her.

"I haven't seen mom this happy since.. ..well, you know. I don't want to think about it. Not today."

I tried to find some way to bring up Wigger, but before I could the sound of spoons banging on glasses arose. Soon the band stopped playing, and the groom stood to give his speech. His bow tie was askew, his ruffled shirt open at the collar. He looked like a movie star poised to accept the Oscar for best marriage.

He waited for quiet, then began by thanking everyone for joining him and his bride on this joyous occasion, especially those who'd come from distant White Bear.

He nodded in the band's direction, thanked them for the music, and asked as a special favor if they'd refrain from stealing the silverware. Polite laughter. He said he hoped the best man got a chance to prove it. More titters. He looked a little embarrassed, like he had to say these kind of things but wished he didn't.

Then my heart, and the hearts of everyone there—even the stone-faced Ervines—went out to him, because emotion overcame Bobby as he spoke of his sorrow over the empty chair at his family's table (actually it wasn't empty, Cuhulain was in it).

"This is all for him," said Bobby, with a sweep of the hand that encompassed the food, the music, the marriage, in one gesture. The look on Betty's face was bittersweet. Her lips trembled as her son paused to compose himself.

"To Bobby Tuttweiler Sr." he said.

Cuhulain hoisted his glass and led a loud, unanimous "AYE!" Bobby left the dais to a round of applause, and went over and kissed his mother.

An Ecclesiastical Matter

Islacked off after the reception. With or without Sean filling in the blanks I felt I could wrap this case up soon, but Eddy G assured me that his release was in the works. I used that as an excuse to let it ride.

Slapper Doran pestered me to join him every time I walked into Tin Cup's. Had I spoken to my pal? How was the case coming? "Siddown siddown, McDonough," he said. "Howsabout a drink?"

One evening I succumbed to his blandishments. It turned out to be interesting, because a couple of his boxers were discussing the finer points of the sport.

Myron Sullivan had a predictable take. I'd seen him fight once. He seemed to possess a barely controlled fury that built on itself when he landed a blow. Thus, his style was one of constant probing and sudden, vicious flurries.

"Ye're always attackin'," he said, "even when yer defendin' yer lookin for an openin', and then y'go after it."

He demonstrated, clenching his fists and his jaw, and bobbing back from a phantom blow with a snarl on his face that must have disheartened all but the bravest of opponents.

Doran's middleweight, Harry Cassidy, told him he ought to learn to counterpunch.

"I tried doin' that," Sullivan said. "Remember, Slapper, down in Omaha?"

Doran nodded with a sour look. "How could I forget?"

They told the tale of that fight, interrupting each other to embellish on a disaster that had begun with such great promise.

"I hit him with a right in the first round, his knees buckled," said Sullivan. "He was out on his feet," said Doran. "We rode the blinds down there," Sullivan explained, "took two days. I thinks to myself, 'I come all this way in a boxcar t'fight thirty seconds? 'C'mon, c'mon,' I sez to him, 'wake up!'"—"'Take him out,' I sez," said Doran, "but My, he wants to practice some moves, use this kid for a punchin' bag. Not smart."—"I couldn't get that feel back," said Sullivan, "couldn't get goin', must'a been the fourth or fifth, I thinks to myself, 'you could lose this one ye damn fool.'"—"It was too late by then," Doran said. "T'my mind it was a close fight but they home-towned us, gave the other guy every round but the first."

He wagged a finger at his boys. "If yez got it in yer hand, take it goddam it!"

I rang Russ the moment I woke up next morning. It had been days since the wedding reception but it sounded like he'd been waiting for my call ever since.

"Why don't you come by right now?" he said.

I gulped a coffee and walked down Rice Street to St. Albert's. Russ was outside the rectory waiting for me, puffing on a fag. "Come on in to the office," he said.

We trod the echoing granite hallway to his little sanctum. It was cozy and highly personalized, with a shelf full of poetry books and lots of plaques and framed photos on all the walls. Another shelf held softball and bowling trophies for parish teams. One plaque, from The Stahl House Winter League, was inscribed to Father Krause personally. He'd won a Turkey Tournament.

The wall behind his desk was devoted to photos of Russ with the great and near great—Mayor Mahoney, the late Governor Olson, Babe Ruth, Bronko Nagurski, some nobodies from local sports and politics.

He seated me in a leather chair and grabbed a bottle of whiskey out of his desk drawer. Over the course of the next hour we had a couple drinks, and a wide ranging conversation. He filled me in on Bobby, gave me lots of useful information about the case, and straightened out an ecclesiastical matter that helped make the pieces fit.

After that we discussed things that had nothing to do with Bobby's murder. By the time our meeting was over I'd decided Russ was an odd and interesting sort of cleric. When I told him I had to go we shook hands, and he wished me luck.

"One more question," I said, as we walked down the hall. "Do you have faith?"

"Not much, how about you?"

"None," I replied.

"Oh, come on. Don't tell me you're not a little intrigued by the mystery. Everybody is.—'tho' he is under, the world's splendor and wonder, His mystery must be stressed—A poet said that."

"I'm a little intrigued by the mystery," I admitted. "Sometimes."

"Then you're just exactly like me."

"That's not very comforting, Russ, you being a priest and all."

"There's not much comfort to be had, Martin."

The Fatal Thing

The temperature was close to 100 and the sky was ominous the next day, when I met Marcie to wrap things up. I parked, and looked down University Avenue. A great wall of cloud was advancing from the west, rolling and billowing, black as a thunderstorm but looming up from the ground, not down from the sky. A rim of sunlight was visible above, a stiff wind blew out ahead. There was enough static electricity in the air to make my skin tingle. I grabbed for my hat. Suddenly the air was thick with little stinging particles. By the time they started pelting me I'd reached The Criterion, and it was a good thing too. By then you couldn't see your hand in front of your face.

I had all I could do to pull the door open against the wind. It banged closed again loudly. A thick haze entered with me. I must've been quite a sight emerging from a cloud, puffs of dust rising from my hat as I whacked it against my knee. The waiter and the bar man both smiled. A few bar flies took note, but most of them never looked up.

It was hot inside, but the fans helped a little. The waiter seated me in a back booth, near one of the solitary middle-aged dames who frequented the place.

I was later than usual. Not as late as Marcie though. She'd sounded hesitant when I called, in sharp contrast to her eagerness to get together earlier. I ordered a cold beer and wondered whether she was just reluctant to close the coffin on her father, or if she didn't want our relationship—such as it was—to end. Or if she wished it was over already.

****

After a few minutes passed and no Marcie I started going through what I'd learned again. Just to make sure.

"I'm on pins and needles," Russ had exclaimed, as soon as I sat down. "Who killed Bobby?"

I told him that it appeared to be a young man he knew.

"Jesus!" He whistled softly. "Who?"

I told him I needed more information before I could be certain, which was why I had to ask him some questions.

"Ok, I'm all ears," he said.

"You knew Bobby pretty well, didn't you?"

He nodded, with a wistful smile. "I heard his confessions often through the years, but our relationship went beyond that. Bobby became comfortable with me as a spiritual advisor."

Russ explained that Bobby's confessions presented a challenge of rare directness, because along with the usual venalities he always had dozens of adulterous encounters to divulge.

"I don't mind telling you that, because I'm sure it won't come as any surprise," he said. "The first time I heard him, I thought this was a man who hadn't confessed for months, maybe years, but it wasn't so. He came back a couple weeks later with the same story to tell." He gave me a sly grin, and stroked his goatee. "The same count, as it were."

According to Russ, he and Bobby did the standard confessor/confesser dance for awhile, pretending they didn't know who'd been on the other side of the curtain, but that didn't last.

"He had a kind of sparkle in his eyes when we ran into each other," said Russ. "Maybe I did too. I was curious. It wasn't long before he began dropping by and talking more informally. So we spent a lot of time together, right here in this office. I thought to myself, this is damned interesting, from a lot of different perspectives. It was a pastoral challenge, it was a glimpse into a unique personality. But most of all, he told some wonderful stories. Love stories."

That came as a shock to my delicate sensibilities. I'd scoffed when Eddy G told me Holy Mother was the only comfort we had, but I still occasionally took solace in the knowledge that something stood between me and the void, something personified by the priesthood and expressed in the ancient rituals, none of which included sitting around and shooting the bull about extra-marital affairs with your confessor.

It was about then that I noticed that the wall of photos behind Russ illustrated more than his meetings with celebrities over the years. It documented his evolution from Father Krause—a conventional-looking young priest with an innocent face and a beatific smile—to a middle-aged wolf named Russ.

"We talked a lot about temptation," Russ continued, "and of course my attitude was the Church's attitude: Temptation is simply there to be resisted, as a sort of moral exercise. I remember the time we first discussed it at length. He was sitting in the chair where you're sitting now. He'd just been to confession a few days before. He'd told me again about the liaisons he'd had outside his marriage. I'd chastised him about his adulterous ways. He took it in good spirit—Bobby always had a good spirit, God bless him—but that day I finally said, "you're just going to keep on doing this, aren't you?'—'Yes, I think I am,' he told me. 'I can see the wisdom of stopping but I'm not sure I can. In fact I'm pretty sure I can't.'

"We just looked at each other and laughed," said Russ.

According to Russ, their dialogue went on until Bobby was murdered. Bobby asked the same questions I might have if I were in his shoes. If God doesn't want you to make love to women, why does he make them so beautiful? Why do they smell so good? Why do they squirm the way they do when you kiss their neck?

"These were things that, to be honest, I wasn't acquainted with," said Russ. "He made them sound pretty good."

"So what'd you decide?"

"I can't say we decided anything, not in the sense that we came to an agreement. I was the one who was supposed to have an answer, but instead Bobby put a question in my mind that I have yet to resolve."

Bobby, Russ explained, didn't agree that temptation always leads to sin. He admitted that some temptations might, but he wondered how you'd know which ones did if you never succumbed to any of them? In other words, how would you know right from wrong? He told Russ that he'd rarely felt wrong after he made love to a woman.

"He knew it corrupted his marriage," said Russ, "but he considered that his wife's failing, or perhaps a failing of the institution itself."

"But he personally never bumped up against a temptation that led him to mortal sin?"

"I didn't say that."

Hints and intimations were all he'd ever gotten from Bobby on that matter, but enough for him to draw some conclusions.

"If you can honestly tell me it would aid your investigation I'll tell you what he did," Russ said.

"Just tell me how you absolved him if he didn't confess."

Russ smiled. "I enjoy a good conversation, and this is about as good as I've had since Bobby was killed.—I take it you aren't observant, but think back to when you were. Didn't you have to ask forgiveness? Of course you did. Now Bobby never asked forgiveness for anything except the most mundane and venial transgressions. Certainly not for seductions and adulteries."

Nevertheless, Russ could tell that he felt pretty bad about the matter they were discussing, bad enough so he wanted to work something out. Not absolution maybe, but some kind of redemption.

And that was how the fatal thing was set in motion.

****

BANG!—The sound of the Criterion's door blowing closed interrupted my recollection. The bar flies' heads all turned. Marcie was wearing a billowy summer dress that fluttered in the breeze from the fans, and those same high-heeled sandals she'd removed the last time we got together. She had a straw sun bonnet in her hand.

She put it on the table, then sat down and fussed with the ribbons.

"Dust storm over?" I asked.

She shook her head no, and studied the bonnet. I studied the tiny beads of sweat on her chest, amongst which perched her pince nez.

"So, who killed him?" she asked.

"I guess we're gettin' right down to work then."

Her eyes crinkled a little. "Maybe I'll have a Manhattan. Just one."

"For old time's sake?"

She eyed me skeptically. "Jeez, Martin, we're not lovers."

"Almost."

She dismissed that notion with a wave of her hand, and ordered a Manhattan. I swallowed a pill with a sip of beer. She asked what it was. I showed her the packet.

"'Carter's Little Liver Pills'? Why not just drink less?"

I said I'd take that under advisement. She scoffed. "A gal would be a fool to get interested in you, Martin. You practically drink for a living."

"You're a little quicker to order a drink than you used to be, I've noticed."

"Huh," she sniffed.

"It's got nothing to do with you though," she added, in a tone that told me it had plenty to do with me, but I didn't know what. I was pretty obtuse in those days.

"I drink for lotsa reasons," I said, "but when I drink with coppers I'm drinkin' for a living. Remember the first time we got together, I told you most murder cases aren't solved? Not precisely true. Most murder cases don't result in a conviction, but the coppers know who the killer is, they just can't prove it. They're usually happy to tell me after a few drinks though."

"Does Eddy Guilfoyle know who killed my father?" she asked.

"Yeah, but he wouldn't say. I had to figure it out. Keep in mind what I just told you though. They know, but they can't prove it, meaning they can't bring enough evidence to the D A to make a case."

I let that sink in, then began to walk her through my investigation.

"The fact that you hired me put a lot of things in motion," I explained.

I began with Eddy's trumped-up cocaine ring. I discovered how completely that had fallen apart the evening I had to tussle to keep Slapper Doran and his boxers from hoisting me on their shoulders and singing, "For He's A Jolly Good Fellow."

It seemed the charges against Slapper had been reduced to misdemeanor possession, which meant that he might cool his heels in the workhouse for a few weeks, but hard time wasn't in the cards. I didn't bother mentioning that I hadn't yet spoken to anyone on his behalf. Thus grows the legend of Martin McDonough, string puller.

I looked for Eddy G amid the clamor of praise and the thrusting of drinks upon my worthy self, but he was nowhere to be seen, so I surrendered to the spirit of the moment.

The morning after I awoke with the usual headache, and the feeling that I should get downtown fast if I wanted to talk to Sean. Nevertheless, I'd arrived too late. I learned something I never would have guessed though. Turns out that the penalty for not being a member of an imaginary nose candy ring in the Saintly City is deportation. Maybe it just applies to smokes.

I told Marcie that Sean's departure left only one alleged conspirator under lock and key. She didn't know where all this was going, of course. She listened patiently, interrupting only to make a few remarks about Eddy's detective work. Corruption was the theme of those comments.

The way she brushed me off when I said we'd almost been lovers, then as much as called me a terminal soak, must've irritated me. I couldn't resist a rejoinder.

"I see now why you're so down on corruption," I told her. "Something pretty rotten led to your father's murder."

"What d'you mean?"

"This case is a strange one, Marcie. It was from the beginning. For instance, I've never been in an investigation where the people who claim to want the truth were so unwilling to give me information. You wouldn't even tell me who you thought was guilty, remember?"

"Yeah, and I told you why.‟

"The rest of your family wouldn't give me anything either. I barely talked to your brother. Your sister told me nothing. I didn't get much from your mother, just a little tip about roses when she described the funeral, unintentional but useful, because later I come to find out that your father's special passion was roses."

Her eyes narrowed. "He was in the flower business, Martin. He liked flowers."

"But roses best of all," I insisted. "Preferably clutched in the trembling hand of a sixteen year old girl.'"

Marcie sighed, and took a sip of her Manhattan.

"Her name was Trudy," she said. "She was so sweet and pretty. So meek."

"I heard you were a friend of hers."

She shrugged, just a little twitch of the shoulders that jiggled her pince nez. "Not really," she said. "She was a poor kid, went to St. Albert's, lived down by the shop ponds. I didn't pay much attention to her. I remember once in school she called me 'Miss Tuttweiler.' I said, 'you can call me Marcella, Trudy.' I suppose she thought that made us friends."

"How'd you find out?"

"She told me. She was proud of it."

"Did she tell other people?" I asked.

"No. I said it had to be our secret.—Why are we talkin' about this, Martin? It happened a long time ago. I hired you to find things out, so I can't complain if they're things I'd sooner you didn't know. But don't tell me Trudy killed him. I don't believe it."

I assured her I wouldn't, and explained how the act of contrition Bobby and Father Russ devised came to involve Danny Wegleitner.

Russ had been proud to tell me that he and Bobby had figured out a way to let some of the "less fortunate" kids in the parish earn some money. He'd directed my attention to the wall of photos behind me, and invited me to take a closer look at some pictures of outings Russ had taken, groups of three or four boys.

There were shots of them canoeing down Phalen Creek, seated in the bleachers at a Saints game, eating candy floss at Como Park, hunting grouse.

****

Those kids were fatherless for the most part," Russ said. "When they were youngsters I tried to give them some of the experiences they might have had otherwise, but by the time Bobby and I worked out the arrangement I'm speaking of they were older, and frankly, with the Depression on, poverty was their main problem. Bobby agreed to put them to work selling roses. You've probably seen them. They stand on busy corners and come around to the bars. There are lots of them now, but it began with just a few, and they were all from this parish."

"Most of the ones I see are girls, Russ. They're sixteen or so."

He nodded. "Correct."

We both knew what he meant.

I peered at the photos closely. He pointed out a picture of a crowded toboggan about to launch down a snowy hill.

"I took this a few years before Bobby and I got to know each other well. That's Bobby, kneeling on the back, under that parka. Bobby Jr. is one of the kids on the toboggan. I got Bobby involved with these kids early on. It was never any kind of quid pro quo at that point, just something I asked him and a lot of parish dads to do. Bobby was always willing."

I asked if there were any photos of Danny Wegleitner.

"Yes." He pointed to one of a boy on a playground swing. "That was about twelve years ago. Here he is when he's older."

I recognized him in that one, a tall, strapping kid, who'd just whacked a softball, and was watching it soar as he dropped the bat and began to stride toward first.

"That your suspect?" Russ asked.

"Yeah."

He sighed. "I was hoping that wasn't the case. He's been in trouble all his life. Bobby's daughter wrote to him when he was in prison, through a program we set up here at the parish. But why would he kill Bobby?"

"Just a guess, but I think Bobby knew he and Angie were getting cozy, and didn't like it."

He sighed. "He wouldn't have. He was determined his children would marry well." He shook his head sadly. "Much as I liked Bobby, loved him really, I feel sorry for

Danny. He's in jail now, you know. At least he was until yesterday."

"He's out?"

Not exactly, Russ explained. He'd visited Danny a few times since his arrest, and he'd gone downtown to do so the day before, but was told that Danny had been transferred. They were holding him in the insane asylum, down in St. Peter.

That came as quite a surprise to me. Russ too. He said Danny had always been in one scrape or another, but he wasn't bugs.

Marcie was skeptical when I told her about Wigger. "Why would he kill my father if he's not nuts?" Marcie asked.

"Good question. I never could answer it. I first suspected him for the same reason Eddy suspected Sheldon Slansky. He's a good suspect. He's been in serious trouble. He did business with your father, could have come knockin' on his door. And he's a cocaine addict. That stuff makes people do funny things."

"Like murder?"

I put my finger to my lips and nodded in the direction of the lady in the nearby booth.

"Y'know, I wondered about that myself," I said. "It's one form of dissipation I have no experience with at all. I had to rely on a musician I ran into at Kuby's. He seemed to know quite a bit about 'snow birds.'"

****

The jailer told me Sean had been hustled out shortly before I'd arrived, with a ticket for the 9:30 train to Chicago and a police escort to make sure he used it. I made it to Union Depot with minutes to spare, risked life and limb flying down the long stairway to the platform just in time to see the bulls put him aboard.

I boarded as well, and caught up before he found a seat.

He was unshaven, and wearing a shirt that looked like it had been crumpled in the bin behind the booking desk since his arrest, but seemed none the worse otherwise. He didn't notice me approaching him, but the conductor did. He was a large fellow with a grin a mile wide and hard eyes that belied it.

"What'chu want!" he demanded. He put a powerful squeeze on my arm.

Sean looked up. "Ah my gumshoe friend," he said, beaming. "This man's ok, Jay-Jay," he told the conductor, who immediately loosened his grip and went about his business.

"Talk amongst the oxford gray back in the slammer had you strivin' to gain my release," he said.

"Simple justice, not to mention the fact that you might be able to help me out."

"ALL ABOARD," shouted the conductor.

I said I realized it was a longshot, but would he wrack his brain anyway, and try to remember if there was anything unusual going on the night before Bobby's murder? Of course he couldn't. He didn't even recall how long ago it had occurred. I told him Bobby was killed on May 25th last year.

"Night before would've been Friday," I said. "Did Wigger do anything special Friday nights? I mean to get ready to sell flowers on Saturday."

"Far's I can remember every night was the same. Wigger'd be around the bar, maybe sittin' at a table for awhile, an' sooner or later him'n Tipper, and that rich gal would go on out n'snort snow. Many nights I walked past'em after the joint closed, after the band had a drink. There they was, sittin' in that big Packard'a hers."

"You'd never talk to'em?"

"Hell no, they busy chinnin' an carryin' on amongst themselves. As is the snow bird's wont."

"What happened the night Tipper died?"

"Like I tole'ya, he jus' went away and never come back. Bobby went lookin' for him, said he wasn't nowhere around. Bobby wasn't into the snow, and he worried 'bout his friends who were."

"And that was after his dad was murdered?"

"Yeah, they was fireworks an' such goin' off. Musta been right roun' the fourth of July.—I heard Bobby married that rich gal. That true?"

"Yeah." I told him about the wedding. "That band needs you in the worst way," I said.

"Looks like they gonna hafta t'do without me." He grinned that tombstone grin of his. "Can't say I'm gonna miss this town."

There was a lurch, the cars banged together, and we were moving. I wished him luck and made it off the train before it passed the platform.

****

Marcie wondered what light my talk with Sean shed on her father's murder. Again, nothing specific, I had to tell her. "But that was a tight little group of hop heads, and there was another good suspect among'em."

"So you're not sure Wigger killed him?"

"Fact is, I'm sure he didn't."

When Russ assured me that Wigger was sane, I'd asked how he knew. He explained that he'd dealt with many troubled kids over the years. "You can tell when they're wrong in the head," he said. "Take this one, for example."

He pointed to a photo of three boys kneeling in a field of corn stubble. Russ and another man were standing behind them, holding a string hung with a brace of quail. One of the boys had a shotgun cradled in the crook of his arm. Russ tapped his finger on the kid with the shotgun.

"He was off his nut," Russ said. "An orphan. He lived with his aunt. She came to me when he was about eleven, told me he'd killed her cat, and she was afraid of him.— Eleven years old and a grown woman was afraid of him. I did what I could, thought maybe hunting might be a way to harness whatever screwy thing about animals was going on in his mind, but he just got odder and odder. Liked to hang around cemeteries, and eventually -"

"Wait a minute. Are you gonna tell me he died in a cemetery?"

"Yes, how did you know?"

"Heard about it at Kuby's. What was his name?"

"Kurt Terwilliger. The boys called him 'Tipper,' because he tipped over gravestones. That was how he died. Tipped a big monument over on himself."

"Sold roses, did he?"

"You could hardly call it selling in his case," Russ explained. "He'd just stand there and hope somebody would ask to buy one.—You're thinking maybe he killed Bobby?"

"Well, he'd have had the same opportunity that Danny Wegleitner did. In any case, I need to talk to Danny,"

According to Russ, that wouldn't be easy. He'd poked around enough to discover that anyone but immediate family needed permission to visit an inmate at St. Peter and it took weeks, even for a priest.

Before we parted we agreed that we'd both try to find a way to short circuit that process.

Marcie said she remembered Tipper the same way Angie did. Strange but harmless.

"Dad and my brother would go on parish outings with the poor kids, and he was one of 'em. He liked my dad. Why would he kill him?"

"Money? There wasn't much at stake, but this kid relied on those roses for whatever cash he had. They were supposed to get old roses from retail florists, but they were getting harder to sell. A source tells me they were always bothering your dad for fresher blooms."

I could see this didn't impress her much motive-wise.

"Tipper's hopped-up, he's not hittin' on all eight. Get it? Don't think of it as an ordinary knockover."

She was skeptical. I told her I didn't blame her, but if we assumed Tipper shot her father, some other things fell into place as well.

"One of them being an aspect of the case that I spoke about too soon," I said. "Your mother did end up with that insurance money."

She looked shocked, but she listened intently while I explained. She knew of her mother's relationship with Cuhulain, and seemed relieved when I told her the route the money took into her mother's hands.

"I suspected she got it," she said. "I asked her, 'ma, do you need some money?' awhile ago and she said she didn't. To be honest, that's when I decided to hire you. I was worried sick, thinkin' why doesn't she? It wasn't because dad put a bunch away, that's for sure. I didn't think she shot him, but —well, you know."

"You were worried she might've had him rubbed out.— No. It came as a complete surprise to her when Cuhulain gave her the money."

"You know that for a fact?"

"Yes."

She took another sip of her Manhattan, heaved a big sigh and relaxed visibly. But the wheels were still going around. I let them turn for awhile.

"But what does her getting the money have to do with that kid killing my dad?"

"Let's backtrack a little. We agreed that we don't believe in coincidences, right? Well, a couple of 'em bother me still. For instance, there were two investigators who looked into this case, me and Eddy Guilfoyle. Your sister started vampin' me the moment I laid eyes on her, and -

"WHAT!"

The woman in the nearby booth turned with a look of frank anticipation on her face.

"Careful," I whispered.

"Why that conniving little flirt," Marcie muttered.

That rock of hers bobbed and sparkled as she drummed her fingers on the table .

"You're the only one gets to tease me, right?"

"I never— How can you say that?"

"Anyway, Angie wasn't teasin.' I know when a gal's struttin' some serious stuff." I leaned in and spoke softly. "She was tryin' to seduce me. And your mother seduced Eddy Guilfoyle."

I sat back and watched her reaction, which was sheer incredulity.

"That's right. Two investigators, your mother seduces one, your sister tries to seduce the other. Is that a co-incidence? Don't get me wrong, I'm not one to minimize my animal magnetism, but the guy Angie'd been vampin' before we got together was more her age, more her type. That'd be Wigger, by the way. And as far as Eddy and your mother are concerned, what's goin' on there?—Sheldon Slansky thought it was Eddy's nose she couldn't resist."

Marcie's nose wrinkled in disgust. "Oh, this is from him, huh? He's still the best suspect as far as I'm—"

"I checked with Eddy, Marcie. He admitted it, gave me details. Wanna hear'em?"

She glanced over at the next booth. "No, unless it has something to do with the murder."

"It does. Why do you think she screwed him?"

Marcie finished her drink and sat quietly for a few moments. This was all coming a little too fast for her. Understandably. It had taken me a couple weeks to sort it out, with the information accumulating slowly, one piece at a time.

She took a deep breath and spoke quietly. "Because she wanted him to keep his mind on the case. She wanted him to arrest Slansky. She thought it would help her get her hands on the money, so she could age with some dignity."

"Want another drink?"

"No. That wouldn't be a good idea."

I said her theory of why her mother seduced Eddy was like a lot of things in this case. It made perfect sense until you probed a little. Then it fell apart. I explained that Faennis Cuhulain made sure he could bestow the cash upon her mother, along with a bouquet of flowers, on the first day of spring.

"Flowers and gifts on the first day of spring are a tradition in the part of Ireland he comes from," I said, "and Cuhulain's a sentimental ham. Eddy Guilfoyle, on the other hand, is not sentimental. He's religious. He thinks it's a sin to make love to a woman outside the sacrament of marriage, and a most grievous sin to do it on Ash Wednesday. He told me the mark of the ash was still on his forehead when your mother seduced him. See the problem there?"

"No."

"Should'a paid more attention to your catechism. Ash Wednesday is a moveable feast. I checked with Father Russ when it fell last year. March 28th, a week after Cuhulain gave her the dough."

I gave her a moment to ponder that.

"So what's your mother's motive?" I asked. "I told you Slansky's theory about his nose, but you're not buyin' it, right?"

"Stop playin' games, Martin. What?"

"Eddy might be corrupt but he's a good investigator," I told her. "I'd be a fool to think that he didn't find out everything I did, a long time ago. The reason it didn't come out is because your mother has been using her wiles on him ever since the murder. At first she really thought Slansky killed your father. So did Eddy, but the closer he looked the less likely that became. Your mother wheedled and pleaded and said she'd end up in the poorhouse, but Eddy knew Slansky didn't kill him, and so did your mother by a couple months after the murder. She persuaded Eddy to ignore what he'd discovered and pretend that Slansky was the only suspect. The longer that went on the more it wore on Eddy. Your mother could see that, and eventually, out of desperation, she seduced him, so she'd have something on him. She really needed him to keep his mouth shut."

"But why is she protecting Tipper?"

"She isn't. The coppers, the crowd at Kuby's, they all say that Tipper tipped an 800 pound monument over on himself, but how would a person do that? It's impossible. Eddy knows it, and if he was interested in solving Tipper's murder he'd know how to start. He'd look for somebody with motive and opportunity."

"Who?"

"Well, he knows what I know, that your brother went lookin' for Tipper in the cemetery the night he died. My guess, when Bobby found him he was workin' on that big stone. Bobby helped him, and made sure it fell the wrong way. Then he told his mother what he'd done."

That stunned her. She said nothing for awhile.

"My brother killed that boy because he killed my father?"

"Makes sense. It's the most common motive for murder."

"What is? Revenge"

"No, love."

There were tears this time, but they were quiet and discreet. The lady who'd been eavesdropping didn't even notice. After awhile Marcie dabbed at her eyes, and asked if I was certain.

I told her one loose end needed tying up, but I knew how we could take care of it. Russ had made some inquiries since we'd met. He'd discovered that a fifty buck bribe paid to the administrator of the St. Peter Asylum would buy the three of us an hour of privacy with Wigger. Russ would gladly hear his confession, and we'd be free to ask him anything we wanted.

"Even if he didn't do it, he knows what happened," I explained. "Otherwise your sister wouldn't have vamped him, and Eddy wouldn't have put him in the frame. It's up to you whether we talk to him. Far as I'm concerned, I've done what you hired me to do. Tipper shot your father.

That's a mortal cinch. If I was in your shoes, I'd consider letting it go at that."

I knew she wouldn't. She gave me the cash and told me to set it up.

Mystery

I'm dredging up the trip to St. Peter seven years later, out of an impaired memory, so I can't vouch for the accuracy of my tale. I'm tempted to call that a sobering thought, but if so it hasn't worked yet.

I have a mental image of Russ seated in the front seat next to the chauffeur, gabbing over his shoulder at Marcie and me about the landscape. According to him, we were in the valley of an ancient river that was five miles wide, and hundreds of feet deep. Its' source, he said, was a gigantic lake formed by a melting glacier, with a massive wall of melting ice at its north shore, and a notch in the hills along the south shore that released the torrent he described.

It was the stuff of dreams, and I dozed as we bumped along a gravel road that mirrored the meandering of the Minnesota River, a placid stream that still flowed although the glacier that once fed it was long gone.

It seemed to me that Marcie was glad to be distracted from the task at hand. She was full of questions for Russ, about glaciers, rivers, geological time. He was happy to fill her in, although he admitted that much of what he described was the result of his own cogitations, inspired by a sense of mystery and a few facts that he'd learned from a book. He knew how to tell a story though.

The trip to the asylum—it was about sixty miles south of St. Paul—took more than three hours. We stopped in a small town about half way. The chauffeur removed a hamper that Marcie had packed for the occasion from the rumble seat, and we had a lunch in a park. She spread a linen cloth on a picnic table and poured us Manhattans from an insulated jug—cold, easy on the Vermouth, not too diluted by the ice cubes. When we finished those she passed around watercress sandwiches.

While Marcie and Russ chatted and put things away, the chauffeur and I took a walk around the park. I asked if he'd driven Marcie to our meetings.

"Yes sir," he replied. "I drive them everywhere. Madam does not drive. Mr. Kirkwood does, but prefers not to."

He told me that he'd routinely waited outside the Criterion while we discussed the case, although the meeting before last she'd sent him home when he dropped her off.

"She said you'd be bringing her back, and indeed you did sir. Earlier than she'd anticipated."

****

The asylum was situated on the bluffs outside town, three brick buildings of Victorian severity. After we parked Marcie took me aside.

"Before we go in there, tell me about this loose end we're tying up." She could see I was hesitant. "C'mon Martin, this is no time to hold out."

"Ok. Maybe it's nothin', but it bothers me. There's this little group of three snow birds, hung around whiffin snow, gabbin' and carryin' on, gettin' to know each other's business. Only one of'em killed your father, but whatever there is to know about that crime all three of'em knew it, and look what's happened to'em.—Tipper's dead. Bobby killed him. That's one."

"I guess so," she agreed.

"Then, months later, after I begin pokin' around, Wigger is arrested with a little nose candy. Not much of a charge, but Eddy claims he's the top guy in a dope ring, and starts arrestin' other people to make the case. Looks like Wigger's goin to the big house. But after I stick my nose in, that falls apart. Next day Wigger is whisked off to an insane asylum. Turns out he's bugs, so anything he might tell the coppers about your father's murder is easily discredited. That's two people who know about the murder and they're silenced, correct?"

"Well, yeah."

Two outta three, leavin' Kate Ervine, who's been vampin' Bobby without makin' any headway. Then, a few weeks ago, outta the clear blue sky, he proposes to her. So what does that sound like to you?"

She thought for a few moments.

"Well, it sounds to me like Eddy Guilfoyle made sure Bobby wouldn't go to trial for killing Tipper."

"And ..."

"And..?"

"C'mon, think about it. Why did Bobby marry Kate?"

"That's easy. To honor dad's wishes."

"Uh-uh. Bobby honored your father the only way he knew how, by imitating him. By makin' time with beautiful women."

She looked skeptical. "Kate isn't beautiful."

"Correct."

She still didn't get it. At first.

"Ahh," she finally said. "You think he married her so she'd couldn't be pressured to testify if he did go to trial."

"Yes. Bobby's head over heels over this gorgeous dame, they're practically livin' as man and wife under your mother's roof, then he decides to marry someone else, someone he isn't much interested in, but she's stuck on him, and might get vindictive and rat if she doesn't get her way. Makes perfect sense, doesn't it?"

She agreed it did, and turned to head for the nuthouse, but I stopped her.

"Problem is, it only makes sense until you think about the crime Bobby committed."

It took a moment for her to see what I was driving at.

"Oh, I guess it would be one of those 'know but can't prove' cases, wouldn't it," she said.

"Correct. There were only two people who knew what happened in that cemetery and one of'em is dead. All your brother had to do is clam up. He'd be a very sympathetic defendant, not the kind a D A wants to put in front of a jury without hard evidence or a confession."

"Bobby doesn't know that."

"Maybe not, but Eddy does. So why did he go to such great lengths to keep Bobby outta the picture?"

She started to ponder that question, but Russ, who was waiting for us at the door, motioned for us to hurry.

We signed in at the administration desk. An officer with a night stick escorted us over to Building B, where Doctor Ecklund, a tall, bald-headed fellow wearing a white jacket and wire-rimmed spectacles, was waiting outside. The doc gave us a quick once-over. Russ's garb was priestly. No question Marcie was a woman. That left me.

"You must be the detective I spoke with," he said, and extended his hand for a shake. I crossed his palm with the agreed upon sum, and he ushered us through the heavy metal door without further formality.

We entered an area about the size of a high school gym. It had the same high windows a basement gym might have too, but these windows were striped with iron bars. Slats of sunlight poured through into an otherwise ill-lit and fetid space; hot, damp, and thick with unpleasant smells.

"Wait here," said the doctor. "Don't be afraid. They won't harm you."

"They" were about a dozen inmates wearing shoes without laces and loose blue shifts, shuffling around in a slow, clockwise circle. They stared at the floor as they walked, but somehow managed to avoid bumping into each other. Most of them were women. A few had tiny pointed heads.

Sounds drifted through the dense air, shrieks, laughter, other unidentifiable noises. The room was like an echo chamber.

A relatively normal looking fellow sat on a bench against the wall, counting imaginary money and piling it up beside him. He shuffled phantom bills off a thick wad, pausing occasionally to lick his thumb. When a pile got high enough to become precarious he'd pat it carefully, then start another. Suddenly he swept the piles to the floor and put head in his hands. His shoulders shook as he wept, but that only lasted a few moments. Then he sat up and started counting again.

One of the pin head women hoisted her shift, squatted, and pissed on the floor.

Marcie reached for my hand. Russ crossed himself. I fixed my eyes on a blackboard on the wall. It was full of "cranial measurements" and scrawled observations: "23 1/4 by 13 3/8—inordinate appetite; 21 by 11.9—wet, filthy agitated; 25.2 by 14—phrenzied, thinks family's been murdered."

The doc reappeared with Wigger, who was in shackles and handcuffs. He motioned for Russ, and the three of them went back down the corridor.

Soon the doc came out again, and engaged us in some small talk about his work.

"I'm a professor of phrenology," he said. "We're correlating symptoms with skull size here, and making great strides I'm proud to say. This is the exercise area. They all get an hour of exercise daily. Well, not all of them. The criminally insane are locked in cells, and in restraints. This is quite a privilege for Mr. Wegleitner, coming out and talking to you. He's been looking forward to it."

He gabbed on but I barely heard him. Marcie squeezed my hand. Soon Russ came out, looking grim. He motioned for us. We dodged the shuffling inmates, stepped carefully around the puddle of pee, and walked down the corridor to an open door.

Wigger was seated at a table, a gasper in his cuffed hand. He was inhaling it with the gusto of a hungry man eating lunch. He took a final drag and dropped the butt. His shackles rattled when he crushed it.

"How'ya doin?" I asked.

"You kiddin?" he replied.

I told him that he didn't strike me as nuts. He said he would be soon enough.

"Got a cigarette?" he asked.

Marcie volunteered to go get one from Russ. I tried a little small talk while she was gone. He was polite, but pretty subdued.

"You're Angie's sis, aint'cha," he said, when Marcie returned.

She nodded yes, and put the cigarette in his mug. I lit a match for him.

"What do you think you're doin' here?" I asked.

He said it had taken him awhile to figure that out. He was so used to being arrested on one thing or another— "suspicion" usually—that he put the whole thing off to bad luck, even after he heard that Slapper Doran was going to finger him, and Sean had been arrested.

"See, I figure Sean's a dinge, so that's why they jammed him. Didn't know about Slap, maybe somethin' between him and that copper with the beak. But after awhile I begin t'thinkin, it ain't got nothin' t'do with snow. It's all just a way to shut me up...."

He looked over at Marcie. "Bobby rubbed Tipper out y'know. Pushed that stone over on him."

Marcie bit her lip.

"Why'd he do it?" I asked.

"Because Tipper killed my dad, right?" said Marcie.

He took a few more drags and looked down at the table.

"Tell us why," she said calmly.

"Tipper'd fit right in here, y'know," he said. "'Bout half'a everything he said was just squirrel talk."

Marcie was looking at him intently. He paused and averted his gaze.

"We was all together up t'this place Kate rented, t'keep her snow at," he continued. "Me, Tipper, Kate, Bobby.— See, Kate was always after Bobby t'come up there after the bar closed, but he never would. Angie did sometimes, but not him, so I was kinda surprised when he came that night. Was a Friday, see, an' next morning me'n Tipper was gonna go get some roses from your dad, but we was up late sniffin' an' drinkin', an' Bobby got this idea that we should play a joke on his old man. See, we was always botherin' your dad for fresh roses, and he was always sayin' no. So Bobby sez, 'let's all go see him tomorrow morning, only Tipper, you bring the shotgun under your coat. You guys ask him for the fresh roses, an' when he says no, stick the gun in his face an' get t'hollerin' at him, scare him good.' Sounded kinda squirrely t'me, but I didn't say nothin, just went along. So next mornin' Tipper was supposed to wake me up, but he never did. Just the two of'em, him and Bobby, went for the flowers."

He took a long pull on his gasper, and sat silently for a few moments.

"C'mon, Danny," Marcie urged. "Tell me what happened."

"So that's what they done. Least that's what Tipper told me. Bobby, he waited down the street. Tipper knocked on the door, an' when your dad opened it he pulls the shotgun an' says, 'go on now, get me some fresh flowers fr' a change!' Your dad musta been scared, so he goes into the cooler to get'em, and by the time he come out Bobby was right there next to Tipper, and he says, 'go on, stick that gun under his chin and shoot him.' An' Tipper says he just done it. Cuz he always done what Bobby said."

"You believe him?" I asked.

He shrugged. "Guess so. I didn't say nothin' for a long time, but when Tipper got squashed, I asked Bobby about it. He said it weren't true, that it was just Tipper talkin loony. 'Bullshit,' I sez. 'You told him to shoot your old man, then you killed him to shut him up, didn't't'cha?' He sez to me, 'now it's you talkin' loony.'"

Marcie was surprisingly calm. "But why would Bobby kill dad?" she asked.

"Beats me. Your dad was a good man. Gave me a job, only one I ever had. I thought the world'a him. So'd Bobby. Didn't he?—I think that copper is takin' care of Bobby. I never would'a peached on him though. I ain't no rat."

Marcie sighed. She patted his cuffed hands.

"Does Angie know?" she asked.

"She sure does, maam. She was kinda givin' me the third degree one time, t'see if I knew. We talked about it. Then she was my squeeze for a bit. That didn't last though. I didn't wanna think she was doin' it to keep me quiet."—He looked over and gave me a rueful little smile. "But when you started snoopin' around she went right after you, didn't she?"

"Yeah. I guess she did," I said.—"One more thing before we go. Where'd you get the snow you were sellin'?"

"Cribbed it from Kate. We was always goin' up t'her place and snortin.' She had so much she couldn't keep track of it."

I told him I'd do what I could to get him out. He thanked me, but didn't seem optimistic.

None of us spoke until we were well on the way back, but when we did, we spoke as if the chauffeur wasn't there. I remember thinking how odd that was. I said that in my opinion what Wigger told us had the ring of truth. Marcie didn't argue.

"I thought my brother was a poet," she said.

"Nah, your father was a poet. Your brother's just a mimic."

We were silent again for awhile.

"Know any poems?" Marcie asked.

"How's about this," I replied: "'Love can make you drink and gamble, make you stay out all night long, love can make you do things that you know are wrong.'"

"That's more of a song," Marcie observed, reasonably.

"Songs are poetic," I said.

"But they're not poems. You know a poem, Father Krause?"

"Call me 'Russ,' dear. Yes I know a few:

'Come gather round me, Parnellites,

And praise our chosen man;

Stand upright on your legs awhile,

Stand upright while you can,

For soon we lie where he is laid,

And he is underground;

Come fill up all those glasses

And pass the bottle round.

"That's more like it," Marcie said. "That's a poem."

Later she wondered aloud how you could love someone and not love him, maybe even hate him, at the same time. It didn't sound that unusual to me. Russ called it a mystery. He said people spent too much time trying to solve mysteries.

"I've learned to cherish them," he told us.

"I hope that attitude doesn't catch on," I said.

Which made Marcie smile.

I was drafted six years later. Now I'm stationed at Camp Gilroy, in California. We do a little drill, peel potatoes, police the area for litter. My buddy, Benny, a student of these things, is giving two to one odds that sometime next year we'll be heading for a well-defended beach on the coastal plain of Japan. Meanwhile, we rarely have that first drink until five P.M. and generally nod out before Taps. I spend hours reminiscing about old cases. My fellow soldiers are fascinated.

St. Paul seems far away. It won't be the same when I go back, I can tell from the only contact I have with the place, the Sunday paper that arrives in the mail the following Friday. No more gangsters, no more bent coppers, lots of sanctimonious crooks who call themselves "public servants," and lots of low-paid divorce work for the likes of me. It's all there if you read between the lines. Times have changed.

The paper keeps me up on people too. The obituaries are good that way. I read where Leon Gleeman was on his way home from downtown when an odd thing happened. He drove directly into a bridge abutment under Kellogg Boulevard, and died instantly. Maybe he had a stroke or something.

Betty Tuttweiler died too, in '43, not young certainly, but she did love hard and leave a good-looking corpse, as the rest of that saying goes.

The Lucky Dog's luck ran out at Anzio, which saddened me, and prompted me to shuffle through the whole deck of might've-beens again.

Shortly after we visited St. Peter I got together with Eddy G. and the two of us decided on the appropriate penalty for not belonging to a nose candy ring, and not being nuts either. Exile solved everyone's problem, we agreed, and he arranged it the next day. I assume Wigger jumped the blinds, rode out the Great Depression and maybe even evaded the draft that way.

Bobby is living happily ever after, but he'll always be Junior.

Eddy admitted that he knew Bobby killed Tipper, and why. We discussed the tactics he'd employed to protect him, dispassionately, like a couple old pros.

"I hadda put the Wegleitner kid in the squeeze," Eddy said.

"He was born in the squeeze," I observed. "He told me he'd never rat, and I don't think he would've."

Eddy was silent on that point, which I took as agreement. He called Bobby a stargazer and a pretty boy, said he wanted to collar him for both murders, even got excited telling me how the D A might have convicted him.

"We wouldn't have stood a chance on either one alone, but using one as evidence for the other? Maybe."

In the end though, the hold Betty had on him stopped him. The conflict between that and his duty made him dread getting up in the morning. He said he felt like he was plodding through sucking mud all day.

"Ever interest you who was sellin' snow in Kuby's?" I asked.

"Not much."

As long as coppers like Eddy are in charge there will never be a shortage of drugs in St. Paul. They find such things so distasteful they ignore them. It's another form of *corruption*.

One afternoon awhile ago I got so bored waiting for the witching hour that I paged through the Society section of a month old Pioneer Press, and happened upon a small item of great personal interest. It said that the recently-widowed Marcella Kirkwood, White Bear, had funded a foundation and named it after her late husband. Among other good works, it would strive to better the lives of those confined to insane asylums. Her good friend and advisor, Father Krause, on leave from St. Albert's, would serve as chief executive officer.

Well, what could I do at that late date except commend Russ's initiative? And hope his service is satisfactory.

As for me, Marcie and Margaret Thornton were the only women I ever considered jumping off the deep end with, and I never laid a finger on either of them. Pathetic as that seems, maybe it's better so. They roam my imagination unsullied, and I'm free to pursue my real interests, such as they are.

Calumet Editions
Proudly Presents

BLOOD

The next Martin McDonough novel
by Bruce Rubenstein.
Coming soon.

Turn the page for a preview of
BLOOD

BLOOD

It could have been worse. If things had worked out differently, there might have come a time when I was involved with both of them at once. I know about a guy who got in that situation and regretted it.

I was reminded of him on one of the bleaker nights of my life, in February 1942.

I was standing on the Union Depot platform in St. Paul, waiting for a troop train. It was almost midnight. I put my back to the frigid west wind, and looked down the tracks for an engine light. Seeing none, I meandered over to the stairway that led back up to the concourse, and all that was warm and familiar. There was nothing to prevent me from climbing those stairs, but I didn't know when the train was coming, and I'd been warned that if I missed it I was "subject to discipline," so instead I ducked into the alcove at the bottom of the stairs and stood there shivering like a dumb beast in the chute.

Out on the platform, snowflakes blew through a halo of light that was cast by a bare bulb swinging in the wind.

I'd aged in lockstep with the twentieth century, which should've put me beyond reach of the draft board, but it was barely eight weeks after Pearl Harbor and Uncle Sam was scraping the bottom of the barrel. Hence my second career as cannon fodder.

I was overdue for a change anyway. The layover was a relic of the past. The gangsters who'd taken advantage of it were dead or in prison. A few has-beens were spending their dotage in the leftover haunts, bowling alleys mostly. The Green Lantern had closed after Harry Sawyer retired to Florida. I was still a Tin Cup's regular, but my real chums were married and staying home nights. The coppers who frequented the joint were younger than me. I didn't take the trouble to cultivate their friendship. Sometimes they gave me information anyway, for what it was worth (nothing to them, I didn't even buy drinks). I gathered they'd have gladly been on the take, but no one was giving.

Everything was falling apart. People were double-crossing each other left and right. The Italian mob could have muscled in any time they wanted to. They didn't bother.

Time had passed me and the city of my birth by so thoroughly that I'd taken to sulking. I'd socked away plenty during my hay-day, so I rarely troubled with the kind of low end work that came my way. Instead I priced myself into early retirement. Instead of arriving at Tin Cup's at a civilized hour, say 4:00 PM, I started dropping in after lunch and heading back to Mrs. Dunn's a few hours later. It was a routine I'd seen many an old-timer adopt. I might have sunk into it for good. Then my draft notice arrived.

It was a shock, but nothing compared to the blow to my system after I joined a few hundred other GI's at Fort Snelling, for a hurry-up version of basic training. The Sergeant, a loud, stupid little dago from out east, announced that there was no hooch allowed on base, and he meant it. By 9 February I'd been without a drink for two weeks. The shakes had calmed to the point where I could hit the target, if not the bullseye.

After I regained the gift of gab (sort of, it surprised me how much of my personality I owed to hooch) I told my fellow draftees I'd been a private eye. From then on they peppered me with questions whenever there was a down moment.— Meet a lot of beautiful women? How about gangsters? Ever kill a man?

It helped me sort out the past, even prompted me to ponder the future. Assuming I had one. There was talk of our imminent deployment, either to England where an army was of invasion was massing, or to the Pacific, where bloody battles were about to be fought. Neither seemed like a survival strategy, but it was out of my control. I would lie down on my bunk after a day of drilling to the soundtrack of our brainless Sergeant barking orders, and envision myself in a scene from a different movie: Me and a bunch of other GI's at a canteen in a train station, some easy-on-the-eye WACs handing out donuts and coffee, a fellow hoocher passing me a flask. That first taste burning my gullet.

Imagine my surprise when Sergeant gate-mouth bellowed my name one evening, while I was in the midst of that very fantasy.

"MAC—DONNA!" he screamed. "PUT'CHA KIT TUGETHAH! YA GOIN' ALL DA WAY!"

"Where?" I managed to ask.

"TA DA STATION, YA DUMB BASTUD! WHERE ELSE!"

I threw some clean underwear into a duffel, shook a few hands, and walked out of the barracks. My fellow trainees looked on in envy. "They're gonna put'ya in Intelligence cuz you was a detective," said one of them. I just shrugged, and climbed into a waiting jeep.

If the driver knew anything he didn't let on. This was part of the plan. No one outside of the brass knew where I was going, but I was given to understand that it was absolutely imperative that I get there. It was as if a top secret scheme to invade France had been hatched, and I'd been picked to lead it.

Later I learned that all over the country that evening they were plucking men like me out of basic, in order to create a battalion of duffers called the "Home Guard." We would soon form into platoons, and be stationed near the coasts. Our duty was to protect the "home front." If there was a softer assignment in the history of warfare I've never heard of it, but as I waited for the troop train that night I was heading toward an uncertain fate.

"Catch the westbound,," said the driver when he dropped me. "Don't know when it's comin' so you'd better stay on the platform. If you miss it you're subject to discipline. Got it?

"And give this to the commanding officer on board," he added. "Don't open it."

He handed me an envelope, which I tore open the moment I entered the depot. It was an incomprehensible jumble of letters and numbers.—I pondered that word, 'discipline,' briefly. Our nitwit Sergeant was always threatening us with the brig, and during the First World War, when I was an impressionable youth, I'd heard that they shot deserters. All things considered, a cold wait for the train seemed best.

I'd been down in the alcove about half an hour when another fellow joined me. He'd been jeeped in from somewhere in Wisconsin with the same mysterious orders, but whoever sent him was a little more forthcoming about the schedule.

"Train's due pretty quick," he informed me.

His name was Milo Bradich. He told me he'd left his wife and two daughters behind on 40 acres that they'd managed to hang on to through the Depression. Now, just when things were looking up, he'd have to rely on hired help to run it. He worried if the men who were available, 50 and older most of them, would be able to bring in a crop, and if they'd be honest if they did. He fretted about his 14 year old daughter's welfare without a father around, whether his wife could hold things together, if there'd be anything left when he got back.

"You married?" he asked.

"Nah, gave it some thought once or twice. Never fit in with the rest of my life."

I told him I was a private eye, worked nights, spent too much time in the joints and in the company of loose women.

"Private eye, huh." He nodded as if he understood.

We heard a whistle off in the distance. It seemed to be coming from the east, so we shouldered our duffle bags and walked out on the platform.

"Ever kill a man?" he asked.

"Yeah."

Soon a light appeared, became brighter, and turned the falling snow into an all-encompassing, white glow. The locomotive chuffed to a halt. Behind it we heard the ponderous thump of cars banging together one after another for what seemed like miles.